IN THE DARK BEFORE DAWN

In Part 1, Stephen King introduced us to Cold Mountain Penitentiary, and the lonely stretch of cells known as the Green Mile. There we met Paul Edgecombe, a guard assigned to watch over the inmates of Death Row. With the arrival of John Coffey, a hulking man convicted of killing two little girls, that cast of the condemned was completed.

In Part 2, we met the other convicts, Eduard Delacroix and William "Billy the Kid" Wharton, who, with Coffey, filled out a twisted triangle of death. But the Green Mile changed when a lone, squeaky mouse gnawed through barriers between guard and inmate to bring them together in a sense of wonder that warmed even this chill place.

In Part 3, the mystery of the fearful John Coffey deepened, as the murderously huge hands of this mountain of a man seemed to work miraculous cures. Was this unspeakable slayer a son of Satan or a saint in devilish disguise?

In Part 4, we walked the Green Mile step by scary step with a man whose most terrible fears did not even come close to matching a fate worse than death itself, as Cold Mountain shook with horrifying screams, and hearts of stone began to melt.

Now prepare yourself for the next spine-chilling chapter. . . .

The Green Mile:

Nigh

STEPHEN KING

The Green Mile

PART FIVE

Night Journey

A SIGNET BOOK

SIGNET
Published by the Penguin Group
Penguin Books USA Inc., 375 Hudson Street,
New York, New York 10014, U.S.A.
Penguin Books Ltd, 27 Wrights Lane,
London W8 5TZ, England
Penguin Books Australia Ltd, Ringwood,
Victoria, Australia
Penguin Books Canada Ltd, 10 Alcorn Avenue,
Toronto, Ontario, Canada M4V 3B2
Penguin Books (N.Z.) Ltd, 182–190 Wairau Road,
Auckland 10, New Zealand

Penguin Books Ltd, Registered Offices:
Harmondsworth, Middlesex, England

First published by Signet, an imprint of Dutton Signet,
a division of Penguin Books USA Inc.

First Printing, July, 1996
10 9 8 7 6 5 4 3 2

PUBLISHER'S NOTE
This is a work of fiction. Names, characters, places, and incidents either
are the product of the author's imagination or are used fictitiously,
and any resemblance to actual persons, living or dead, events, or locales
is entirely coincidental.

1

Mr. H. G. Wells once wrote a story about a man who invented a time machine, and I have discovered that, in the writing of these memoirs, I have created my own time machine. Unlike Wells's, it can only travel into the past—back to 1932, as a matter of fact, when I was the bull-goose screw in E Block of Cold Mountain State Penitentiary—but it's eerily efficient, for all that. Still, this time machine reminds me of the old Ford I had in those days: you could be sure that it would start eventually, but you never knew if a turn of the key would be enough to fire the motor, or if you were going to have to get out and crank until your arm practically fell off.

I've had a lot of easy starts since I started telling the story of John Coffey, but yesterday I had to crank. I think it was because I'd gotten to Delacroix's execution, and part of my mind didn't want to have to relive that. It was a bad death, a *terrible* death, and it happened the way it did because of Percy Wetmore, a young man who loved to comb his hair but couldn't stand to be laughed at—not even by a half-bald little Frenchman who was never going to see another Christmas.

As with most dirty jobs, however, the hardest part is just getting started. It doesn't matter to an engine whether you use the key or have to crank; once you get it going, it'll usually run just as sweet either way. That's how it worked for me yesterday. At first the words came in little bursts of phrasing, then in whole sentences, then in a torrent. Writing is a special and rather terrifying form of remembrance, I've discovered—there is a totality to it that seems almost like rape. Perhaps I only feel that way because I've become a very old man (a thing that happened behind my own back, I sometimes feel), but I don't think so. I believe that the combination of pencil and memory creates a kind of practical magic, and magic is dangerous. As a man who knew John Coffey and saw what he could do—to mice and to men—I feel very qualified to say that.

Magic is dangerous.

In any case, I wrote all day yesterday, the words simply flooding out of me, the sunroom of this glorified old folks' home gone, replaced by the storage room at the end of the Green Mile where so many of my problem children took their last sit-me-downs, and the bottom of the stairs which led to the tunnel under the road. That was where Dean and Harry and Brutal and I confronted Percy Wetmore over Eduard Delacroix's smoking body and made Percy renew his promise to put in for transfer to the Briar Ridge state mental facility.

There are always fresh flowers in the sunroom, but

by noon yesterday all I could smell was the noxious aroma of the dead man's cooked flesh. The sound of the power mower on the lawn down below had been replaced by the hollow plink of dripping water as it seeped slowly through the tunnel's curved roof. The trip was on. I had travelled back to 1932, in soul and mind, if not body.

I skipped lunch, wrote until four o'clock or so, and when I finally put my pencil down, my hand was aching. I walked slowly down to the end of the second-floor corridor. There's a window there that looks out on the employee parking lot. Brad Dolan, the orderly who reminds me of Percy—and the one who is altogether too curious about where I go and what I do on my walks—drives an old Chevrolet with a bumper sticker that says I HAVE SEEN GOD AND HIS NAME IS NEWT. It was gone; Brad's shift was over and he'd taken himself off to whatever garden spot he calls home. I envision an Airstream trailer with *Hustler* gatefolds Scotch-taped to the walls and Dixie Beer cans in the corners.

I went out through the kitchen, where dinner preparations were getting started. "What you got in that bag, Mr. Edgecombe?" Norton asked me.

"It's an empty bottle," I said. "I've discovered the Fountain of Youth down there in the woods. I pop down every afternoon about this time and draw a little. I drink it at bedtime. Good stuff, I can tell you."

"May be keepin you young," said George, the other cook, "but it ain't doin *shit* for your looks."

We all had a laugh at that, and I went out. I found myself looking around for Dolan even though his car was gone, called myself a chump for letting him get so far under my skin, and crossed the croquet course. Beyond it is a scraggy little putting green that looks ever so much nicer in the Georgia Pines brochures, and beyond that is a path that winds into the little copse of woods east of the nursing home. There are a couple of old sheds along this path, neither of them used for anything these days. At the second, which stands close to the high stone wall between the Georgia Pines grounds and Georgia Highway 47, I went in and stayed for a little while.

I ate a good dinner that night, watched a little TV, and went to bed early. On many nights I'll wake up and creep back down to the TV room, where I watch old movies on the American Movie Channel. Not last night, though; last night I slept like a stone, and with none of the dreams that have so haunted me since I started my adventures in literature. All that writing must have worn me out; I'm not as young as I used to be, you know.

When I woke and saw that the patch of sun which usually lies on the floor at six in the morning had made it all the way up to the foot of my bed, I hit the deck in a hurry, so alarmed I hardly noticed the arthritic flare of pain in my hips and knees and ankles. I dressed as fast as I could, then hurried down the hall to the window that overlooks the employees' parking lot, hoping the slot where Dolan parks his old Chevrolet would still be empty. Sometimes he's as much as half an hour late—

No such luck. The car was there, gleaming rustily in the morning sun. Because Mr. Brad Dolan has something to arrive on time for these days, doesn't he? Yes. Old Paulie Edgecombe goes somewhere in the early mornings, old Paulie Edgecombe is up to something, and Mr. Brad Dolan intends to find out what it is. *What do you do down there, Paulie? Tell me.* He would likely be watching for me already. It would be smart to stay right where I was ... except I couldn't.

"Paul?"

I turned around so fast I almost fell down. It was my friend Elaine Connelly. Her eyes widened and she put out her hands, as if to catch me. Lucky for her I caught my balance; Elaine's arthritis is terrible, and I probably would have broken her in two like a dry stick if I'd fallen into her arms. Romance doesn't die when you pass into the strange country that lies beyond eighty, but you can forget the *Gone with the Wind* crap.

"I'm sorry," she said. "I didn't mean to startle you."

"That's all right," I said, and gave her a feeble smile. "It's a better wake-up than a faceful of cold water. I should hire you to do it every morning."

"You were looking for his car, weren't you? Dolan's car."

There was no sense kidding her about it, so I nodded. "I wish I could be sure he's over in the west wing. I'd like to slip out for a little while, but I don't want him to see me."

She smiled—a ghost of the teasing imp's smile she must have had as a girl. "Nosy bastard, isn't he?"

"Yes."

"He's not in the west wing, either. I've already been down to breakfast, sleepyhead, and I can tell you where he is, because I peeked. He's in the kitchen."

I looked at her, dismayed. I had known Dolan was curious, but not how curious.

"Can you put your morning walk off?" Elaine asked.

I thought about it. "I *could*, I suppose, but . . ."

"You shouldn't."

"No. I shouldn't."

Now, I thought, *she'll ask me where I go, what I have to do down in those woods that's so damned important.*

But she didn't. Instead she gave me that imp's smile again. It looked strange and absolutely wonderful on her too-gaunt, pain-haunted face. "Do you know Mr. Howland?" she asked.

"Sure," I said, although I didn't see him much; he was in the west wing, which at Georgia Pines was almost like a neighboring country. "Why?"

"Do you know what's special about him?"

I shook my head.

"Mr. Howland," Elaine said, smiling more widely than ever, "is one of only five residents left at Georgia Pines who have permission to smoke. That's because he was a resident before the rules changed."

A grandfather clause, I thought. And what place was more fitted for one than an old-age home?

She reached into the pocket of her blue-and-white-striped dress and pulled two items partway out: a cigarette and a book of matches. "Thief of green, thief of red," she sang in a lilting, funny voice. "Little Ellie's going to wet the bed."

"Elaine, what—"

"Walk an old girl downstairs," she said, putting the cigarette and matches back into her pocket and taking my arm in one of her gnarled hands. We began to walk back down the hall. As we did, I decided to give up and put myself in her hands. She was old and brittle, but not stupid.

As we went down, walking with the glassy care of the relics we have now become, Elaine said: "Wait at the foot. I'm going over to the west wing, to the hall toilet there. You know the one I mean, don't you?"

"Yes," I said. "The one just outside the spa. But why?"

"I haven't had a cigarette in over fifteen years," she said, "but I feel like one this morning. I don't know how many puffs it'll take to set off the smoke detector in there, but I intend to find out."

I looked at her with dawning admiration, thinking how much she reminded me of my wife—Jan might have done exactly the same thing. Elaine looked back at me, smiling her saucy imp's smile. I cupped my hand around the back of her lovely long neck, drew her face to mine, and kissed her mouth lightly. "I love you, Ellie," I said.

"Oooh, such big talk," she said, but I could tell she was pleased.

"What about Chuck Howland?" I asked. "Is he going to get in trouble?"

"No, because he's in the TV room, watching *Good*

Morning America with about two dozen other folks. And I'm going to make myself scarce as soon as the smoke detector turns on the west-wing fire alarm."

"Don't you fall down and hurt yourself, woman. I'd never forgive myself if—"

"Oh, stop your fussing," she said, and this time *she* kissed *me*. Love among the ruins. It probably sounds funny to some of you and grotesque to the rest of you, but I'll tell you something, my friend: weird love's better than no love at all.

I watched her walk away, moving slowly and stiffly (but she will only use a cane on wet days, and only then if the pain is terrible; it's one of her vanities), and waited. Five minutes went by, then ten, and just as I was deciding she had either lost her courage or discovered that the battery of the smoke detector in the toilet was dead, the fire alarm went off in the west wing with a loud, buzzing burr.

I started toward the kitchen at once, but slowly—there was no reason to hurry until I was sure Dolan was out of my way. A gaggle of old folks, most still in their robes, came out of the TV room (here it's called the Resource Center; now *that's* grotesque) to see what was going on. Chuck Howland was among them, I was happy to see.

"Edgecombe!" Kent Avery rasped, hanging onto his walker with one hand and yanking obsessively at the crotch of his pajama pants with the other. "Real alarm or just another falsie? What do you think?"

"No way of knowing, I guess," I said.

Just about then three orderlies went trotting past,

all headed for the west wing, yelling at the folks clustered around the TV-room door to go outside and wait for the all-clear. The third in line was Brad Dolan. He didn't even look at me as he went past, a fact that pleased me to no end. As I went on down toward the kitchen, it occurred to me that the team of Elaine Connelly and Paul Edgecombe would probably be a match for a dozen Brad Dolans, with half a dozen Percy Wetmores thrown in for good measure.

The cooks in the kitchen were continuing to clear up breakfast, paying no attention to the howling fire alarm at all.

"Say, Mr. Edgecombe," George said. "I believe Brad Dolan been lookin for you. In fact, you just missed him."

Lucky me, I thought. What I said out loud was that I'd probably see Mr. Dolan later. Then I asked if there was any leftover toast lying around from breakfast.

"Sure," Norton said, "but it's stone-cold dead in the market. You runnin late this morning."

"I am," I agreed, "but I'm hungry."

"Only take a minute to make some fresh and hot," George said, reaching for the bread.

"Nope, cold will be fine," I said, and when he handed me a couple of slices (looking mystified—actually both of them looked mystified), I hurried out the door, feeling like the boy I once was, skipping school to go fishing with a jelly fold-over wrapped in waxed paper slipped into the front of my shirt.

Outside the kitchen door I took a quick, reflexive look around for Dolan, saw nothing to alarm me, and hurried across the croquet course and putting green, gnawing on one of my pieces of toast as I went. I slowed a little as I entered the shelter of the woods, and as I walked down the path, I found my mind turning to the day after Eduard Delacroix's terrible execution.

I had spoken to Hal Moores that morning, and he had told me that Melinda's brain tumor had caused her to lapse into bouts of cursing and foul language ... what my wife had later labelled (rather tentatively; she wasn't sure it was really the same thing) as Tourette's Syndrome. The quavering in his voice, coupled with the memory of how John Coffey had healed both my urinary infection and the broken back of Delacroix's pet mouse, had finally pushed me over the line that runs between just thinking about a thing and actually *doing* a thing.

And there was something else. Something that had to do with John Coffey's hands, and my shoe.

So I had called the men I worked with, the men I had trusted my life to over the years—Dean Stanton, Harry Terwilliger, Brutus Howell. They came to lunch at my house on the day after Delacroix's execution, and they at least listened to me when I outlined my plan. Of course, they all knew that Coffey had healed the mouse; Brutal had actually seen it. So when I suggested that another miracle might result if we took John Coffey to Melinda Moores, they didn't outright laugh. It was Dean Stanton who raised the most troubling question: What if John Coffey escaped while we had him out on his field-trip?

"Suppose he killed someone else?" Dean asked. "I'd hate losing my job, and I'd hate going to jail—

I got a wife and kids depending on me to put bread in their mouths—but I don't think I'd hate either of those things near as much as having another little dead girl on my conscience."

There was silence, then, all of them looking at me, waiting to see how I'd respond. I knew everything would change if I said what was on the tip of my tongue; we had reached a point beyond which retreat would likely become impossible.

Except retreat, for me, at least, was already impossible. I opened my mouth and said

2

"That won't happen."

"How in God's name can you be so sure?" Dean asked.

I didn't answer. I didn't know just how to begin. I had known this would come up, of course I had, but I still didn't know how to start telling them what was in my head and heart. Brutal helped.

"You don't think he did it, do you, Paul?" He looked incredulous. "You think that big lug is innocent."

"I'm positive he's innocent," I said.

"How *can* you be?"

"There are two things," I said. "One of them is my shoe."

"Your *shoe*?" Brutal exclaimed. "What has your *shoe* got to do with whether or not John Coffey killed those two little girls?"

"I took off one of my shoes and gave it to him last night," I said. "After the execution, this was, when things had settled back down a little. I pushed it through the bars, and he picked it up in those big hands of his. I told him to tie it. I had to make sure, you see, because all our problem children normally wear is slippers—a man who really wants to commit suicide can do it with shoelaces, if he's dedicated. That's something all of us know."

They were nodding.

"He put it on his lap and got the ends of the laces crossed over all right, but then he was stuck. He said he was pretty sure someone had showed him how to do it when he was a lad—maybe his father or maybe one of the boyfriends his mother had after the father was gone—but he'd forgot the knack."

"I'm with Brutal—I still don't see what your shoe has to do with whether or not Coffey killed the Detterick twins," Dean said.

So I went over the story of the abduction and murder again—what I'd read that hot day in the prison library with my groin sizzling and Gibbons snoring in the corner, and all that the reporter, Hammersmith, told me later.

"The Dettericks' dog wasn't much of a biter, but it was a world-class barker," I said. "The man who took the girls kept it quiet by feeding it sausages. He crept a little closer every time he gave it one, I imagine, and while the mutt was eating the last one, he reached out, grabbed it by the head, and twisted. Broke its neck.

"Later, when they caught up with Coffey, the deputy in charge of the posse—Rob McGee, his name was—spotted a bulge in the chest pocket of the biballs Coffey was wearing. McGee thought at first it might be a gun. Coffey said it was a lunch, and that's what it turned out to be—a couple of sandwiches and a pickle, wrapped up in newspaper and tied with butcher's string. Coffey couldn't remember who gave it to him, only that it was a woman wearing an apron."

"Sandwiches and a pickle but no sausages," Brutal said.

"No sausages," I agreed.

"Course not," Dean said. "He fed those to the dog."

"Well, that's what the prosecutor said at the trial," I agreed, "but if Coffey opened his lunch and fed the sausages to the dog, how'd he tie the newspaper back up again with that butcher's twine? I don't know when he even would have had the chance, but leave that out of it, for the time being. This man can't even tie a simple granny knot."

There was a long moment of thunderstruck silence, broken at last by Brutus. "Holy shit," he said in a low voice. "How come no one brought that up at the trial?"

"Nobody thought of it," I said, and found myself again thinking of Hammersmith, the reporter—Hammersmith who had been to college in Bowling Green, Hammersmith who liked to think of himself as enlightened, Hammersmith who had told me that mongrel dogs and Negroes were about the same, that either might take a chomp out of you suddenly, and for no reason. Except he kept calling them *your* Negroes, as if they were still property ... but not *his* property. No, not his. Never his. And at that time, the South was full of Hammersmiths. "Nobody was really *equipped* to think of it, Coffey's own attorney included."

"But *you* did," Harry said. "Goddam, boys, we're sittin here with Mr. Sherlock Holmes." He sounded simultaneously joshing and awed.

"Oh, put a cork in it," I said. "I wouldn't have thought of it either, if I hadn't put together what he told Deputy McGee that day with what he said after he cured my infection, and what he said after he healed the mouse."

"What?" Dean asked.

"When I went into his cell, it was like I was hypnotized. I didn't feel like I could have stopped doing what he wanted, even if I'd tried."

"I don't like the sound of that," Harry said, and shifted uneasily in his seat.

"I asked him what he wanted, and he said 'Just to help.' I remember that very clearly. And when it was over and I was better, he knew. 'I helped it,' he said. 'I helped it, didn't I?'"

Brutal was nodding. "Just like with the mouse. You said 'You helped it,' and Coffey said it back to you like he was a parrot. 'I helped Del's mouse.' Is that when you knew? It was, wasn't it?"

"Yeah, I guess so. I remembered what he said to McGee when McGee asked him what had happened. It was in every story about the murders, just about. 'I couldn't help it. I tried to take it back, but it was too late.' A man saying a thing like that with two little dead girls in his arms, them white and blonde, him as big as a house, no wonder they got it wrong. They heard what he was saying in a way that would agree with what they were seeing, and what they were seeing was black. They thought he was confessing, that he was saying he'd had a compulsion to take those girls, rape them, and kill them. That he'd come to his senses and tried to stop—"

"But by then it was too late," Brutal murmured.

"Yes. Except what he was *really* trying to tell them was that he'd found them, tried to heal them—to bring them back—and had no success. They were too far gone in death."

"Paul, do you believe that?" Dean asked. "Do you really, honest-to-God believe that?"

I examined my heart as well as I could one final time, then nodded my head. Not only did I know it now, there was an intuitive part of me that had known something wasn't right with John Coffey's situation from the very beginning, when Percy had come onto the block hauling on Coffey's arm and blaring "Dead man walking!" at the top of his lungs. I had shaken hands with him, hadn't I? I had never shaken the hand of a man coming on the Green Mile before, but I had shaken Coffey's.

"Jesus," Dean said. "Good Jesus Christ."

"Your shoe's one thing," Harry said. "What's the other?"

"Not long before the posse found Coffey and the girls, the men came out of the woods near the south bank of the Trapingus River. They found a patch of flattened-down grass there, a lot of blood, and the rest of Cora Detterick's nightie. The dogs got confused for a bit. Most wanted to go southeast, downstream along the bank. But two of them—the coon-dogs—

wanted to go *upstream.* Bobo Marchant was running the dogs, and when he gave the coonies a sniff of the nightgown, they turned with the others."

"The coonies got mixed up, didn't they?" Brutal asked. A strange, sickened little smile was playing around the corners of his mouth. "They ain't built to be trackers, strictly speaking, and they got mixed up on what their job was."

"Yes."

"I don't get it," Dean said.

"The coonies forgot whatever it was Bobo ran under their noses to get them started," Brutal said. "By the time they came out on the riverbank, the coonies were tracking the *killer,* not the girls. That wasn't a problem as long as the killer and the girls were together, but ..."

The light was dawning in Dean's eyes. Harry had already gotten it.

"When you think about it," I said, "you wonder how anybody, even a jury wanting to pin the crime on a wandering black fellow, could have believed John Coffey was their man for even a minute. Just the idea of keeping the dog quiet with food until he could snap its neck would have been beyond Coffey.

"He was never any closer to the Detterick farm than the south bank of the Trapingus, that's what I think. Six or more miles away. He was just mooning along, maybe meaning to go down to the railroad tracks and catch a freight to somewhere else—when they come off the trestle, they're going slow enough to hop—when he heard a commotion to the north."

"The killer?" Brutal asked.

"The killer. He might have raped them already, or maybe the rape was what Coffey heard. In any case, that bloody patch in the grass was where the killer finished the business; dashed their heads together, dropped them, and then hightailed it."

"Hightailed it northwest," Brutal said. "The direction the coon-dogs wanted to go."

"Right. John Coffey comes through a stand of alders that grows a little way southeast of the spot where the girls were left, probably curious about all the noise, and he finds their bodies. One of them might still have been alive; I suppose it's possible both of them were, although not for much longer. John Coffey wouldn't have known if they were dead, that's for sure. All he knows is that he's got a healing power in his hands, and he tried to use it on Cora and Kathe Detterick. When it didn't work, he broke down, crying and hysterical. Which is how they found him."

"Why didn't he stay there, where he found them?" Brutal asked. 'Why take them south along the riverbank? Any idea?"

"I bet he did stay put, at first," I said. "At the trial, they kept talking about a *big* trampled area, all the grass squashed flat. And John Coffey's a big man."

"John Coffey's a fucking giant," Harry said, pitching his voice very low so my wife wouldn't hear him cuss if she happened to be listening.

"Maybe he panicked when he saw that what he was doing wasn't working. Or maybe he got the idea that the killer was still there, in the woods upstream, watching him. Coffey's big, you know, but not real brave. Harry, remember him asking if we left a light on in the block after bedtime?"

"Yeah. I remember thinking how funny that was, what with the size of him." Harry looked shaken and thoughtful.

"Well, if he didn't kill the little girls, who did?" Dean asked.

I shook my head. "Someone else. Someone *white* would be my best guess. The prosecutor made a big deal about how it would have taken a strong man to kill a dog as big as the one the Dettericks kept, but—"

"That's crap," Brutus rumbled. "A strong twelve-year-old girl could break a big dog's neck, if she took the dog by surprise and knew where to grab. If Coffey didn't do it, it could have been damned near anyone ... any man, that is. We'll probably never know."

I said, "Unless he does it again."

"We wouldn't know even then, if he did it down Texas or over in California," Harry said.

Brutal leaned back, screwed his fists into his eyes like a tired child, then dropped them into his lap again. "This is a nightmare," he said. "We've got a man who may be innocent—who probably *is* innocent—and he's going to walk the Green Mile just as sure as God made tall trees and little fishes. What are we supposed to do about it? If we start in with that healing-fingers shit, everyone is going to laugh their asses off, and he'll end up in the Fry-O-Lator just the same."

"Let's worry about that later," I said, because I didn't have the slightest idea how to answer him. "The question right now is what we do—or don't do—about Melly. I'd say step back and take a few days to think it over, but I believe every day we wait raises the chances that he won't be able to help her."

"Remember him holding his hands out for the mouse?" Brutal asked. " 'Give im to me while there's still time,' he said. *While there's still time.*"

"I remember."

Brutal considered, then nodded. "I'm in. I feel bad about Del, too, but mostly I think I just want to see what happens when he touches her. Probably nothing will, but maybe . . ."

"I doubt like hell we even get the big dummy off the block," Harry said, then sighed and nodded. "But who gives a shit? Count me in."

"Me, too," Dean said. "Who stays on the block, Paul? Do we draw straws for it?"

"No, sir," I said. "No straws. You stay."

"Just like that? The hell you say!" Dean replied, hurt and angry. He whipped off his spectacles and began to polish them furiously on his shirt. "What kind of a bum deal is that?"

"The kind you get if you're young enough to have kids still in school," Brutal said. "Harry and me's bachelors. Paul's married, but his kids are grown and off on their own, at least. This is a *mucho* crazy stunt we're planning here; I think we're almost sure to get caught." He gazed at me soberly. "One thing you didn't mention, Paul, is that if we do manage to get him out of the slam and then Coffey's healing fingers don't work, Hal Moores is apt to turn us in himself." He gave me a chance to reply to this, maybe to rebut it, but I couldn't and so I kept my mouth shut. Brutal turned back to Dean and went on. "Don't get me wrong, you're apt to lose your job, too, but at least you'd have a chance to get clear of prison if the heat really came down. Percy's going to think it was a prank; if you're on the duty desk, you can say you thought the same thing and we never told you any different."

"I still don't like it," Dean said, but it was clear he'd go along with it, like it or not. The thought of his kiddies had convinced him. "And it's to be tonight? You're sure?"

"If we're going to do it, it had *better* be tonight," Harry said. "If I get a chance to think about it, I'll most likely lose my nerve."

"Let me be the one to go by the infirmary," Dean said. "I can do that much at least, can't I?"

"As long as you can do what needs doing without getting caught," Brutal said.

Dean looked offended, and I clapped him on the shoulder. "As soon after you clock in as you can . . . all right?"

"You bet."

My wife popped her head through the door as if I'd given her a cue to do so. "Who's for more iced tea?" she asked brightly. "What about you, Brutus?"

"No, thanks," he said. "What I'd like is a good hard knock of whiskey, but under the circumstances, that might not be a good idea."

Janice looked at me; smiling mouth, worried eyes. "What are you getting these boys into, Paul?" But before I could even think of framing a reply, she raised her hand and said, "Never mind, I don't want to know."

3

Later, long after the others were gone and while I was dressing for work, she took me by the arm, swung me around, and looked into my eyes with fierce intensity.

"Melinda?" she asked.

I nodded.

"Can you do something for her, Paul? Really do something for her, or is it all wishful dreaming brought on by what you saw last night?"

I thought of Coffey's eyes, of Coffey's hands, and of the hypnotized way I'd gone to him when he'd wanted me. I thought of him holding out his hands for Mr. Jingles's broken, dying body. *While there's still time*, he had said. And the black swirling things that turned white and disappeared.

"I think we might be the only chance she has left," I said at last.

"Then take it," she said, buttoning the front of my new fall coat. It had been in the closet since my birthday at the beginning of September, but this was only the third or fourth time I'd actually worn it. "Take it."

And she practically pushed me out the door.

4

I clocked in that night—in many ways the strangest night of my entire life—at twenty past six. I thought I could still smell the faint, lingering odor of burned flesh on the air. It had to be an illusion—the doors to the outside, both on the block and in the storage room, had been open most of the day, and the previous two shifts had spent hours scrubbing in there—but that didn't change what my nose was telling me, and I didn't think I could have eaten any dinner even if I hadn't been scared almost to death about the evening which lay ahead.

Brutal came on the block at quarter to seven, Dean at ten 'til. I asked Dean if he would go over to the infirmary and see if they had a heating pad for my back, which I seemed to have strained that early morning, helping to carry Delacroix's body down into the tunnel. Dean said he'd be happy to. I believe he wanted to tip me a wink, but restrained himself.

Harry clocked on at three minutes to seven.

"The truck?" I asked.

"Where we talked about."

So far, so good. There followed a little passage of

time when we stood by the duty desk, drinking coffee and studiously not mentioning what we were all thinking and hoping: that Percy was late, that maybe Percy wasn't going to show up at all. Considering the hostile reviews he'd gotten on the way he'd handled the electrocution, that seemed at least possible.

But Percy apparently subscribed to that old axiom about how you should get right back on the horse that had thrown you, because here he came through the door at six minutes past seven, resplendent in his blue uniform, with his sidearm on one hip and his hickory stick in its ridiculous custom-made holster on the other. He punched his time-card, then looked around at us warily (except for Dean, who hadn't come back from the infirmary yet). "My starter busted," he said. "I had to crank."

"Aw," Harry said, "po' baby."

"Should have stayed home and got the cussed thing fixed," Brutal said blandly. "We wouldn't want you straining your arm none, would we, boys?"

"Yeah, you'd like that, wouldn't you?" Percy sneered, but I thought he seemed reassured by the relative mildness of Brutal's response. That was good. For the next few hours we'd have to walk a line with him—not too hostile, but not too friendly, either. After last night, he'd find anything even approaching warmth suspect. We weren't going to get him with his guard down, we all knew that, but I thought we could catch him with it a long piece from all the way up if we played things just right. It was important that we move fast, but it was also important—to me, at least—that nobody be hurt. Not even Percy Wetmore.

Dean came back and gave me a little nod.

"Percy," I said, "I want you to go on in the storeroom and mop down the floor. Stairs to the tunnel, too. Then you can write your report on last night."

"*That* should be creative," Brutal remarked, hooking his thumbs into his belt and looking up at the ceiling.

"You guys are funnier'n a fuck in church," Percy said, but beyond that he didn't protest. Didn't even point out the obvious, which was that the floor in there had already been washed at least twice that day. My guess is that he was glad for the chance to be away from us.

I went over the previous shift report, saw nothing that concerned me, and then took a walk down to Wharton's cell. He was sitting there on his bunk with his knees drawn up and his arms clasped around his shins, looking at me with a bright, hostile smile.

"Well, if it ain't the big boss," he said. "Big as life and twice as ugly. You look happier'n a pig knee-deep in shit, Boss Edgecombe. Wife give your pecker a pull before you left home, did she?"

"How you doing, Kid?" I asked evenly, and at that he brightened for real. He let go of his legs, stood up, and stretched. His smile broadened, and some of the hostility went out of it.

"Well, damn!" he said. "You got my name right for once! What's the matter with you, Boss Edgecombe? You sick or sumpin?"

No, not sick. I'd *been* sick, but John Coffey had

taken care of that. His hands no longer knew the trick of tying a shoe, if they ever had, but they knew other tricks. Yes indeed they did.

"My friend," I told him, "if you want to be a Billy the Kid instead of a Wild Bill, it's all the same to me."

He puffed visibly, like one of those loathsome fish that live in South American rivers and can sting you almost to death with the spines along their backs and sides. I dealt with a lot of dangerous men during my time on the Mile, but few if any so repellent as William Wharton, who considered himself a great outlaw, but whose jailhouse behavior rarely rose above pissing or spitting through the bars of his cell. So far we hadn't given him the awed respect he felt was his by right, but on that particular night I wanted him tractable. If that meant lathering on the softsoap, I would gladly lather it on.

"I got a lot in common with the Kid, and you just better believe it," Wharton said. "I didn't get here for stealing candy out of a dimestore." As proud as a man who's been conscripted into the Heroes' Brigade of the French Foreign Legion instead of one whose ass has been slammed into a cell seventy long steps from the electric chair. "Where's my supper?"

"Come on, Kid, report says you had it at five-fifty. Meatloaf with gravy, mashed, peas. You don't con me that easy."

He laughed expansively and sat down on his bunk again. "Put on the radio, then." He said radio in the way people did back then when they were joking, so it rhymed with the fifties slang word "Daddy-O."

It's funny how much a person can remember about times when his nerves were tuned so tight they almost sang.

"Maybe later, big boy," I said. I stepped away from his cell and looked down the corridor. Brutal had strolled down to the far end, where he checked to make sure the restraint-room door was on the single lock instead of the double. I knew it was, because I'd already checked it myself. Later on, we'd want to be able to open that door as quick as we could. There would be no time spent emptying out the attic-type rick-rack that had accumulated in there over the years; we'd taken it out, sorted it, and stored it in other places not long after Wharton joined our happy band. It had seemed to us the room with the soft walls was apt to get a lot of use, at least until "Billy the Kid" strolled the Mile.

John Coffey, who would usually have been lying down at this time, long, thick legs dangling and face to the wall, was sitting on the end of his bunk with his hands clasped, watching Brutal with an alertness—a *thereness*—that wasn't typical of him. He wasn't leaking around the eyes, either.

Brutal tried the door to the restraint room, then came on back up the Mile. He glanced at Coffey as he passed Coffey's cell, and Coffey said a curious thing: "Sure. I'd *like* a ride." As if responding to something Brutal had said.

Brutal's eyes met mine. *He knows*, I could almost hear him saying. *Somehow he knows.*

I shrugged and spread my hands, as if to say *Of course he knows.*

5

Old Toot-Toot made his last trip of the night down to E Block with his cart at about quarter to nine. We bought enough of his crap to make him smile with avarice.

"Say, you boys seen that mouse?" he asked.

We shook our heads.

"Maybe Pretty Boy has," Toot said, and gestured with his head in the direction of the storage room, where Percy was either washing the floor, writing his report, or picking his ass.

"What do you care? It's none of your affair, either way," Brutal said. "Roll wheels, Toot. You're stinkin the place up."

Toot smiled his peculiarly unpleasant smile, toothless and sunken, and made a business of sniffing the air. "That ain't me you smell," he said. "That be Del, sayin so-long."

Cackling, he rolled his cart out the door and into the exercise yard. And he went on rolling it for another ten years, long after I was gone—hell, long after Cold Mountain was gone—selling Moon Pies and pops to the guards and prisoners who could afford them. Sometimes even now I hear him in my dreams, yelling that he's fryin, he's fryin, he's a done tom turkey.

The time stretched out after Toot was gone, the clock seeming to crawl. We had the radio for an hour and a half, Wharton braying laughter at Fred Allen and *Allen's Alley*, even though I doubt like hell he understood many of the jokes. John Coffey sat on the end of his bunk, hands clasped, eyes rarely leaving whoever was at the duty desk. I have seen men waiting that way in bus stations for their buses to be called.

Percy came in from the storage room around quarter to eleven and handed me a report which had been laboriously written in pencil. Eraser-crumbs lay over the sheet of paper in gritty smears. He saw me run my thumb over one of these, and said hastily: "That's just a first pass, like. I'm going to copy it over. What do you think?"

What I thought was that it was the most outrageous goddam whitewash I'd read in all my born days. What I told him was that it was fine, and he went away, satisfied.

Dean and Harry played cribbage, talking too loud, squabbling over the count too often, and looking at the crawling hands of the clock every five seconds or so. On at least one of their games that night, they appeared to go around the board three times instead of twice. There was so much tension in the air that I felt I could almost have carved it like clay, and the only people who didn't seem to feel it were Percy and Wild Bill.

When it got to be ten of twelve, I could stand it no longer and gave Dean a little nod. He went into my office with a bottle of R.C. Cola bought off Toot's cart, and came back out a minute or two later. The cola was now in a tin cup, which a prisoner can't break and then slash with.

I took it and glanced around. Harry, Dean, and Brutal were all watching me. So, for that matter, was John Coffey. Not Percy, though. Percy had returned to the storage room, where he probably felt more at ease on this particular night. I gave the tin cup a quick sniff and got no odor except for the R.C., which had an odd but pleasant cinnamon smell back in those days.

I took it down to Wharton's cell. He was lying on his bunk. He wasn't masturbating—yet, anyway—but had raised quite a boner inside his shorts and was giving it a good healthy twang every now and again, like a dopey bass-fiddler hammering an extra-thick E-string.

"Kid," I said.

"Don't bother me," he said.

"Okay," I agreed. "I brought you a pop for behaving like a human being all night—damn near a record for you—but I'll just drink it myself."

I made as if to do just that, raising the tin cup (battered all up and down the sides from many angry bangings on many sets of cell bars) to my lips. Wharton was off the bunk in a flash, which didn't surprise me. It wasn't a high-risk bluff; most deep cons—lifers, rapists, and the men slated for Old Sparky—are pigs for their sweets, and this one was no exception.

"Gimme that, you clunk," Wharton said. He spoke as if he were the foreman and I was just another lowly peon. "Give it to the Kid."

I held it just outside the bars, letting him be the one to reach through. Doing it the other way around is a recipe for disaster, as any long-time prison screw will tell you. That was the kind of stuff we thought of without even knowing we were thinking of it— the way we knew not to let the cons call us by our first names, the way we knew that the sound of rapidly jingling keys meant trouble on the block, because it was the sound of a prison guard running and prison guards *never* run unless there's trouble in the valley. Stuff Percy Wetmore was never going to get wise to.

Tonight, however, Wharton had no interest in grabbing or choking. He snatched the tin cup, downed the pop in three long swallows, then voiced a resounding belch. *"Excellent!"* he said.

I held my hand out. "Cup."

He held it for a moment, teasing with his eyes. "Suppose I keep it?"

I shrugged. "We'll come in and take it back. You'll go down to the little room. And you will have drunk your last R.C. Unless they serve it down in hell, that is."

His smile faded. "I don't like jokes about hell, screwtip." He thrust the cup out through the bars. "Here. Take it."

I took it. From behind me, Percy said: "Why in God's name did you want to give a lugoon like him a soda-pop?"

Because it was loaded with enough infirmary dope to put him on his back for forty-eight hours, and he never tasted a thing, I thought.

"With Paul," Brutal said, "the quality of mercy is not strained; it droppeth like the gentle rain from heaven."

"Huh?" Percy asked, frowning.

"Means he's a soft touch. Always has been, always will be. Want to play a game of Crazy Eights, Percy?"

Percy snorted. "Except for Go Fish and Old Maid, that's the stupidest card-game ever made."

"That's why I thought you might like a few hands," Brutal said, smiling sweetly.

"Everybody's a wisenheimer," Percy said, and sulked off into my office. I didn't care much for the little rat parking his ass behind my desk, but I kept my mouth shut.

The clock crawled. Twelve-twenty; twelve-thirty. At twelve-forty, John Coffey got up off his bunk and stood at his cell door, hands grasping the bars loosely. Brutal and I walked down to Wharton's cell and looked in. He lay there on his bunk, smiling up at the ceiling. His eyes were open, but they looked like big glass balls. One hand lay on his chest; the other dangled limply off the side of his bunk, knuckles brushing the floor.

"Gosh," Brutal said, "from Billy the Kid to Willie the Weeper in less than an hour. I wonder how many of those morphine pills Dean put in that tonic."

"Enough," I said. There was a little tremble in my voice. I don't know if Brutal heard it, but I sure did. "Come on. We're going to do it."

"You don't want to wait for beautiful there to pass out?"

"He's passed out now, Brute. He's just too buzzed to close his eyes."

"You're the boss." He looked around for Harry, but Harry was already there. Dean was sitting bolt-upright at the duty desk, shuffling the cards so hard and fast it was a wonder they didn't catch fire, throwing a little glance to his left, at my office, with every flutter-shuffle. Keeping an eye out for Percy.

"Is it time?" Harry asked. His long, horsey face was very pale above his blue uniform blouse, but he looked determined.

"Yes," I said. "If we're going through with it, it's time."

Harry crossed himself and kissed his thumb. Then he went down to the restraint room, unlocked it, and came back with the straitjacket. He handed it to Brutal. The three of us walked up the Green Mile. Coffey stood at his cell door, watching us go, and said not a word. When we reached the duty desk, Brutal put the straitjacket behind his back, which was broad enough to conceal it easily.

"Luck," Dean said. He was as pale as Harry, and looked just as determined.

Percy was behind my desk, all right, sitting in my chair and frowning over the book he'd been toting around with him the last few nights—not *Argosy* or *Stag* but *Caring for the Mental Patient in Institutions.* You would have thought, from the guilty, worried glance he threw our way when we walked in, that it had been *The Last Days of Sodom and Gomorrah.*

"What?" he asked, closing the book in a hurry. "What do you want?"

"To talk to you, Percy," I said, "that's all."

But he read a hell of a lot more than a desire to talk on our faces, and was up like a shot, hurrying—not quite running, but almost—toward the open door to the storeroom. He thought we had come to give him a ragging at the very least, and more likely a good roughing up.

Harry cut around behind him and blocked the doorway, arms folded on his chest.

"Saaay!" Percy turned to me, alarmed but trying not to show it. "What *is* this?"

"Don't ask, Percy," I said. I had thought I'd be okay—back to normal, anyway—once we actually got rolling on this crazy business, but it wasn't working out that way. I couldn't believe what I was doing. It was like a bad dream. I kept expecting my wife to shake me awake and tell me I'd been moaning in my sleep. "It'll be easier if you just go along with it."

"What's Howell got behind his back?" Percy asked in a ragged voice, turning to get a better look at Brutal.

"Nothing," Brutal said. "Well . . . *this,* I suppose—"

He whipped the straitjacket out and shook it beside one hip, like a matador shaking his cape to make the bull charge.

Percy's eyes widened, and he lunged. He meant to run, but Harry grabbed his arms and a lunge was all he was able to manage.

"Let go of me!" Percy shouted, trying to jerk out of Harry's grasp. It wasn't going to happen, Harry outweighed him by almost a hundred pounds and had the muscles of a man who spent most of his spare time plowing and chopping, but Percy gave it a good enough effort to drag Harry halfway across the room and to rough up the unpleasant green carpet I kept meaning to replace. For a moment I thought he was even going to get one arm free—panic can be one hell of a motivator.

"Settle down, Percy," I said. "It'll go easier if—"

"Don't you tell me to settle down, you ignoramus!" Percy yelled, jerking his shoulders and trying to free his arms. "Just get away from me! All of you! I know people! *Big* people! If you don't quit this, you'll have to go all the way to South Carolina just to get a meal in a soup kitchen!"

He gave another forward lunge and ran his upper thighs into my desk. The book he'd been reading, *Caring for the Mental Patient in Institutions*, gave a jump, and the smaller, pamphlet-sized book which had been hidden inside it popped out. No wonder Percy had looked guilty when we came in. It wasn't *The Last Days of Sodom and Gomorrah*, but it was the one we sometimes gave to inmates who were feeling especially horny and who had been well-behaved enough to deserve a treat. I've mentioned it, I think—the little cartoon book where Olive Oyl does everybody except Sweet Pea, the kid.

I found it sad that Percy had been in my office and pursuing such pallid porn, and Harry—what I could see of him from over Percy's straining shoulder—looked mildly disgusted, but Brutal hooted with laughter, and that took the fight out of Percy, at least for the time being.

"Oh Poicy," he said. "What would your mother say? For that matter, what would the governor say?"

Percy was blushing a dark red. "Just shut up. And leave my mother out of it."

Brutal tossed me the straitjacket and pushed his face up into Percy's. "Sure thing. Just stick out your arms like a good boy."

Percy's lips were trembling, and his eyes were too bright. He was, I realized, on the verge of tears. "I won't," he said in a childish, trembling voice, "and you can't make me." Then he raised his voice and began to scream for help. Harry winced and so did I. If we ever came close to just dropping the whole thing, it was then. We might have, except for Brutal. He never hesitated. He stepped behind Percy so he was shoulder to shoulder with Harry, who still had Percy's hands pinned behind him. Brutal reached up and took Percy's ears in his hands.

"Stop that yelling," Brutal said. "Unless you want to have a pair of the world's most unique teabag caddies."

Percy quit yelling for help and just stood there, trembling and looking down at the cover of the crude cartoon book, which showed Popeye and Olive doing it in a creative way I had heard of but never tried. "Oooh, Popeye!" read the balloon over Olive's head. "Uck-uck-uck-uck!" read the one over Popeye's. He was still smoking his pipe.

"Hold out your arms," Brutal said, "and let's have no more foolishness about it. Do it now."

"I won't," Percy said. "I won't, and you can't make me."

"You're dead wrong about that, you know," Brutal

said, then clamped down on Percy's ears and twisted them the way you might twist the dials on an oven. An oven that wasn't cooking the way you wanted. Percy let out a miserable shriek of pain and surprise that I would have given a great deal not to have heard. It wasn't *just* pain and surprise, you see; it was understanding. For the first time in his life, Percy was realizing that awful things didn't just happen to other people, those not fortunate enough to be related to the governor. I wanted to tell Brutal to stop, but of course I couldn't. Things had gone much too far for that. All I could do was to remind myself that Percy had put Delacroix through God knew what agonies simply because Delacroix had laughed at him. The reminder didn't go very far toward soothing the way I felt. Perhaps it might have, if I'd been built more along the lines of Percy.

"Stick those arms out there, honey," Brutal said, "or you get another."

Harry had already let go of young Mr. Wetmore. Sobbing like a little kid, the tears which had been standing in his eyes now spilling down his cheeks, Percy shot his hands out straight in front of him, like a sleepwalker in a movie comedy. I had the sleeves of the straitjacket up his arms in a trice. I hardly had it over his shoulders before Brutal had let go of Percy's ears and grabbed the straps hanging down from the jacket's cuffs. He yanked Percy's hands around to his sides, so that his arms were crossed tightly on his chest. Harry, meanwhile, did up the back and snapped the cross-straps. Once Percy gave in and stuck out his arms, the whole thing took less than ten seconds.

"Okay, hon," Brutal said. "Forward harch."

But he wouldn't. He looked at Brutal, then turned his terrified, streaming eyes on me. Nothing about his connections now, or how we'd have to go all the way to South Carolina just to get a free meal; he was far past that.

"Please," he whispered in a hoarse, wet voice. "Don't put me in with him, Paul."

Then I understood why he had panicked, why he'd fought us so hard. He thought we were going to put him in with Wild Bill Wharton; that his punishment for the dry sponge was to be a dry cornholing from the resident psychopath. Instead of feeling sympathy for Percy at this realization, I felt disgust and a hardening of my resolve. He was, after all, judging us by the way he would have behaved, had our positions been reversed.

"Not Wharton," I said. "The restraint room, Percy. You're going to spend three or four hours in there, all by yourself in the dark, thinking about what you did to Del. It's probably too late for you to learn any new lessons about how people are supposed to behave—Brute thinks so, anyway—but I'm an optimist. Now move."

He did, muttering under his breath that we'd be sorry for this, plenty sorry, just wait and see, but on the whole he seemed relieved and reassured.

When we herded him out into the hall, Dean gave us a look of such wide-eyed surprise and dewy innocence that I could have laughed, if the business hadn't been so serious. I've seen better acting in backwoods Grange revues.

"Say, don't you think the joke's gone far enough?" Dean asked.

"You just shut up, if you know what's good for you," Brutal growled. These were lines we'd scripted at lunch, and that was just what they sounded like to me, scripted lines, but if Percy was scared enough and confused enough, they still might save Dean Stanton's job in a pinch. I myself didn't think so, but anything was possible. Any time I've doubted that, then or since, I just think about John Coffey, and Delacroix's mouse.

We ran Percy down the Green Mile, him stumbling and gasping for us to slow down, he was going to go flat on his face if we didn't slow down. Wharton was on his bunk, but we went by too fast for me to see if he was awake or asleep. John Coffey was standing at his cell door and watching. "You're a bad man and you deserve to go in that dark place," he said, but I don't think Percy heard him.

Into the restraint room we went, Percy's cheeks red and wet with tears, his eyes rolling into their sockets, his pampered locks all flopping down on his forehead. Harry pulled Percy's gun with one hand and his treasured hickory head-knocker with the other. "You'll get em back, don't worry," Harry said. He sounded a trifle embarrassed.

"I wish I could say the same about your job," Percy replied. "*All* your jobs. You can't do this to me! You *can't!*"

He was obviously prepared to go on in that vein for quite awhile, but we didn't have time to listen to his sermon. In my pocket was a roll of friction-tape, the thirties ancestor of the strapping-tape folks use today. Percy saw it and started to back away. Brutal grabbed him from behind and hugged him until I had slapped the tape over his mouth, winding the roll around to the back of his head, just to be sure. He was going to have a few less swatches of hair when the tape came off, and a pair of *seriously* chapped lips into the bargain, but I no longer much cared. I'd had a gutful of Percy Wetmore.

We backed away from him. He stood in the middle of the room, under the caged light, wearing the strait-jacket, breathing through flared nostrils, and making muffled *mmmph! mmmph!* sounds from behind the tape. All in all, he looked as crazy as any other prisoner we'd ever jugged in that room.

"The quieter you are, the sooner you get out," I said. "Try to remember that, Percy."

"And if you get lonely, think about Olive Oyl," Harry advised. "Uck-uck-uck-uck."

Then we went out. I closed the door and Brutal locked it. Dean was standing a little way up the Mile, just outside of Coffey's cell. He had already put the master key in the top lock. The four of us looked at each other, no one saying anything. There was no need to. We had started the machinery; all we could do now was hope that it ran the course we had laid out instead of jumping the tracks somewhere along the line.

"You still want to go for that ride, John?" Brutal asked.

"Yes, sir," Coffey said. "I reckon."

"Good," Dean said. He turned the first lock, removed the key, and seated it in the second.

"Do we need to chain you up, John?" I asked.

Coffey appeared to think about this. "Can if you want to," he said at last. "Don't *need* to."

I nodded at Brutal, who opened the cell door, then turned to Harry, who was more or less pointing Percy's .45 at Coffey as Coffey emerged from his cell.

"Give those to Dean," I said.

Harry blinked like someone awakening from a momentary doze, saw Percy's gun and stick still in his hands, and passed them over to Dean. Coffey, meanwhile, hulked in the corridor with his bald skull almost brushing one of the caged overhead lights. Standing there with his hands in front of him and his shoulders sloped forward to either side of his barrel chest, he made me think again, as I had the first time I saw him, of a huge captured bear.

"Lock Percy's toys in the duty desk until we get back," I said.

"*If* we get back," Harry added.

"I will," Dean said to me, taking no notice of Harry.

"And if someone shows up—probably no one will, but if someone does—what do you say?"

"That Coffey got upset around midnight," Dean said. He looked as studious as a college student taking a big exam. "We had to give him the jacket and put him in the restraint room. If there's noise, whoever hears it'll just think it's him." He raised his chin at John Coffey.

"And what about us?" Brutal asked.

"Paul's over in Admin, pulling Del's file and going over the witnesses," Dean said. "It's especially important this time, because the execution was such a balls-up. He said he'd probably be there the rest of the shift. You and Harry and Percy are over in the laundry, washing your clothes."

Well, that was what folks said, anyway. There was a crap-game in the laundry supply room some nights; on others it was blackjack or poker or acey-deucey. Whatever it was, the guards who participated were said to be washing their clothes. There was usually moonshine at these get-togethers, and on occasion a joystick would go around the circle. It's been the same in prisons since prisons were invented, I suppose. When you spend your life taking care of mud-men, you can't help getting a little dirty yourself. In any case, we weren't likely to be checked up on. "Clothes washing" was treated with great discretion at Cold Mountain.

"Right with Eversharp," I said, turning Coffey around and putting him in motion. "And if it all falls down, Dean, you don't know nothing about nothing."

"That's easy to say, but—"

At that moment, a skinny arm shot out from between the bars of Wharton's cell and grabbed Coffey's slab of a bicep. We all gasped. Wharton should have been dead to the world, all but comatose, yet here he stood, swaying back and forth on his feet like a hard-tagged fighter, grinning blearily.

Coffey's reaction was remarkable. He didn't pull away, but he also gasped, pulling air in over his teeth like someone who has touched something cold and unpleasant. His eyes widened, and for a moment he looked as if he and dumb had never even met, let alone got up together every morning and lain down together every night. He had looked alive—*there*—when he had wanted me to come into his cell so he could touch me. Help me, in Coffeyspeak. He had looked that way again when he'd been holding his hands out for the mouse. Now, for the third time, his face had lit up, as if a spotlight had suddenly been turned on inside his brain. Except it was different this time. It was *colder* this time, and for the first time I wondered what might happen if John Coffey were suddenly to run amok. We had our guns, we could shoot him, but actually taking him down might not be easy to do.

I saw similar thoughts on Brutal's face, but Wharton just went on grinning his stoned, loose-lipped grin. "Where do you think you're going?" he asked. It came out something like *Wherra fink yerr gone?*

Coffey stood still, looking first at Wharton, then at Wharton's hand, then back into Wharton's face. I could not read that expression. I mean I could see the intelligence in it, but I couldn't *read* it. As for Wharton, I wasn't worried about him at all. He wouldn't remember any of this later; he was like a drunk walking in a blackout.

"You're a bad man," Coffey whispered, and I couldn't tell what I heard in his voice—pain or anger or fear. Maybe all three. Coffey looked down at the hand on his arm again, the way you might look at a bug which could give you a really nasty bite, had it a mind.

"That's right, nigger," Wharton said with a bleary, cocky smile. "Bad as you'd want."

I was suddenly positive that something awful was going to happen, something that would change the planned course of this early morning as completely as a cataclysmic earthquake can change the course of a river. It was going to happen, and nothing I or any of us did would stop it.

Then Brutal reached down, plucked Wharton's hand off John Coffey's arm, and that feeling stopped. It was as if some potentially dangerous circuit had been broken. I told you that in my time in E Block, the governor's line never rang. That was true, but I imagine that if it ever had, I would have felt the same relief that washed over me when Brutal removed Wharton's hand from the big man towering beside me. Coffey's eyes dulled over at once; it was as if the searchlight inside his head had been turned off.

"Lie down, Billy," Brutal said. "Take you some rest." That was my usual line of patter, but under the circumstances, I didn't mind Brutal using it.

"Maybe I will," Wharton agreed. He stepped back, swayed, almost went over, and caught his balance at the last second. "Whoo, daddy. Whole room's spinnin around. Like bein drunk."

He backed toward his bunk, keeping his bleary regard on Coffey as he went. "Niggers ought to have they own 'lectric chair," he opined. Then the backs of his knees struck his bunk and he swooped down onto it. He was snoring before his head touched his thin prison pillow, deep blue shadows brushed under the hollows of his eyes and the tip of his tongue lolling out.

"Christ, how'd he get up with so much dope in him?" Dean whispered.

"It doesn't matter, he's out now," I said. "If he starts to come around, give him another pill dissolved in a glass of water. No more than one, though. We don't want to kill him."

"Speak for yourself," Brutal rumbled, and gave Wharton a contemptuous look. "You can't kill a monkey like him with dope, anyway. They thrive on it."

"He's a bad man," Coffey said, but in a lower voice this time, as if he was not quite sure of what he was saying, or what it meant.

"That's right," Brutal said. "Most wicked. But that's not a problem now, because we ain't going to tango with him anymore." We started walking again, the four of us surrounding Coffey like worshippers circling an idol that's come to some stumbling kind of half life. "Tell me something, John—do you know where we're taking you?"

"To help," he said. "I think . . . to help . . . a lady?" He looked at Brutal with hopeful anxiety.

Brutal nodded. "That's right. But how do you know that? How do you *know*?"

John Coffey considered the question carefully, then shook his head. "I don't know," he told Brutal. "To tell you the truth, boss, I don't know much of anything. Never have."

And with that we had to be content.

6

I had known the little door between the office and the steps down to the storage room hadn't been built with the likes of Coffey in mind, but I hadn't realized how great the disparity was until he stood before it, looking at it thoughtfully.

Harry laughed, but John himself seemed to see no humor in the big man standing in front of the little door. He wouldn't have, of course; even if he'd been quite a few degrees brighter than he was, he wouldn't have. He'd been that big man for most of his life, and this door was just a scrap littler than most.

He sat down, scooted through it that way, stood up again, and went down the stairs to where Brutal was waiting for him. There he stopped, looking across the empty room at the platform where Old Sparky waited, as silent—and as eerie—as the throne in the castle of a dead king. The cap hung with hollow jauntiness from one of the back-posts, looking less like a king's crown than a jester's cap, however, something a fool would wear, or shake to make his high-born audience laugh harder at his jokes. The chair's shadow, elongated and spidery, climbed one wall like a threat. And yes, I thought I could still smell burned flesh in the air. It was faint, but I thought it was more than just my imagination.

Harry ducked through the door, then me. I didn't like the frozen, wide-eyed way John was looking at Old Sparky. Even less did I like what I saw on his arms when I got close to him: goosebumps.

"Come on, big boy," I said. I took his wrist and attempted to pull him in the direction of the door leading down to the tunnel. At first he wouldn't go, and I might as well have been trying to pull a boulder out of the ground with my bare hands.

"Come on, John, we gotta go, 'less you want the coach-and-four to turn back into a pumpkin," Harry said, giving his nervous laugh again. He took John's other arm and tugged, but John still wouldn't come. And then he said something in a low and dreaming voice. It wasn't me he was speaking to, it wasn't any of us, but I have still never forgotten it.

"They're still in there. Pieces of them, still in there. I hear them screaming."

Harry's nervous chuckles ceased, leaving him with a smile that hung on his mouth like a crooked shutter hangs on an empty house. Brutal gave me a look that was almost terrified, and stepped away from John Coffey. For the second time in less than five minutes, I sensed the whole enterprise on the verge of collapse. This time I was the one who stepped in; when disaster threatened a third time, a little later on, it would be Harry. We all got our chance that night, believe me.

I slid in between John and his view of the chair, standing on my tiptoes to make sure I was completely blocking his sight-line. Then I snapped my fingers in front of his eyes, twice, sharply.

"Come on!" I said. "Walk! You said you didn't need to be chained, now prove it! Walk, big boy! Walk, John Coffey! Over there! That door!"

His eyes cleared. "Yes, boss." And praise God, he began to walk.

"Look at the door, John Coffey, just at the door and nowhere else."

"Yes, boss." John fixed his eyes obediently on the door.

"Brutal," I said, and pointed.

He hurried in advance, shaking out his keyring, finding the right one. John kept his gaze fixed on the door to the tunnel and I kept my gaze fixed on John, but from the corner of one eye I could see Harry throwing nervous glances at the chair, as if he had never seen it before in his life.

There are pieces of them still in there . . . I hear them screaming.

If that was true, then Eduard Delacroix had to be screaming longest and loudest of all, and I was glad I couldn't hear what John Coffey did.

Brutal opened the door. We went down the stairs with Coffey in the lead. At the bottom, he looked glumly down the tunnel, with its low brick ceiling. He was going to have a crick in his back by the time we got to the other end, unless—

I pulled the gurney over. The sheet upon which we'd laid Del had been stripped (and probably incinerated), so the gurney's black leather pads were visible. "Get on," I told John. He looked at me doubtfully, and I nodded encouragement. "It'll be easier for you and no harder for us."

"Okay, Boss Edgecombe." He sat down, then lay back, looking up at us with worried brown eyes. His feet, clad in cheap prison slippers, dangled almost all the way to the floor. Brutal got in between them and pushed John Coffey along the dank corridor as he had pushed so many others. The only difference was that the current rider was still breathing. About halfway along—under the highway, we would have been, and able to hear the muffled drone of passing cars, had there been any at that hour—John began to smile. "Say," he said, "this is fun." He wouldn't think so the next time he rode the gurney; that was the thought which crossed my mind. In fact, the next time he rode the gurney, he wouldn't think or feel anything. Or would he? There are pieces of them still in there, he had said; he could hear them screaming.

Walking behind the others and unseen by them, I shivered.

"I hope you remembered Aladdin, Boss Edgecombe," Brutal said as we reached the far end of the tunnel.

"Don't worry," I said. Aladdin looked no different from the other keys I carried in those days—and I had a bunch that must have weighed four pounds—but it was the master key of master keys, the one that opened everything. There was one Aladdin key for each of the five cellblocks in those days, each the property of the block super. Other guards could borrow it, but only the bull-goose screw didn't have to sign it out.

There was a steel-barred gate at the far end of the tunnel. It always reminded me of pictures I'd seen of old castles; you know, in days of old when knights were bold and chivalry was in flower. Only Cold Mountain was a long way from Camelot. Beyond the gate, a flight of stairs led up to an unobtrusive bulkhead-style door with signs reading NO TRES-PASSING and STATE PROPERTY and ELECTRIFIED WIRE on the outside.

I opened the gate and Harry swung it back. We went up, John Coffey once more in the lead, shoulders slumped and head bent. At the top, Harry got around him (not without some difficulty, either, although he was the smallest of the three of us) and unlocked the bulkhead. It was heavy. He could move it, but wasn't able to flip it up.

"Here, boss," John said. He pushed to the front again—bumping Harry into the wall with one hip as he did so—and raised the bulkhead with one hand. You would have thought it was painted cardboard instead of sheet steel.

Cold night air, moving with the ridge-running wind we would now get most of the time until March or April, blew down into our faces. A swirl of dead leaves came with it, and John Coffey caught one of them with his free hand. I will never forget the way he looked at it, or how he crumpled it beneath his broad, handsome nose so it would release its smell.

"Come on," Brutal said. "Let's go, forward harch."

We climbed out. John lowered the bulkhead and Brutal locked it—no need for the Aladdin key on this door, but it was needed to unlock the gate in the pole-and-wire cage which surrounded the bulkhead.

"Hands to your sides while you go through, big fella," Harry murmured. "Don't touch the wire, if you don't want a nasty burn."

Then we were clear, standing on the shoulder of the road in a little cluster (three foothills around a mountain is what I imagine we looked like), staring across at the walls and lights and guard-towers of Cold Mountain Penitentiary. I could actually see the vague shape of a guard inside one of those towers, blowing on his hands, but only for a moment; the road-facing windows in the towers were small and unimportant. Still, we would have to be very, very quiet. And if a car *did* come along now, we could be in deep trouble.

"Come on," I whispered. "Lead the way, Harry."

We slunk north along the highway in a little conga-line, Harry first, then John Coffey, then Brutal, then me. We breasted the first rise and walked down the other side, where all we could see of the prison was the bright glow of the lights in the tops of the trees. And still Harry led us onward.

"Where'd you park it?" Brutal stage-whispered, vapor puffing from his mouth in a white cloud. "Baltimore?"

"It's right up ahead," Harry replied, sounding nervous and irritable. "Hold your damn water, Brutus."

But Coffey, from what I'd seen of him, would have been happy to walk until the sun came up, maybe until it went back down again. He looked everywhere, starting—not in fear but in delight, I am quite sure—when an owl hoo'd. It came to me that, while he might be afraid of the dark inside, he wasn't afraid of it out here, not at all. He was caressing the night, rubbing his senses across it the way a man might rub his face across the swells and concavities of a woman's breasts.

"We turn here," Harry muttered.

A little finger of road—narrow, unpaved, weeds running up the center crown—angled off to the right. We turned up this and walked another quarter of a mile. Brutal was beginning to grumble again when Harry stopped, went to the left side of the track, and began to remove sprays of broken-off pine boughs. John and Brutal pitched in, and before I could join them, they had uncovered the dented snout of an old Farmall truck, its wired-on headlights staring at us like buggy eyes.

"I wanted to be as careful as I could, you know," Harry said to Brutal in a thin, scolding voice. "This may be a big joke to you, Brutus Howell, but I come from a very religious family, I got cousins back in the hollers so damn holy they make the Christians look like lions, and if I get caught playing at something like this—!"

"It's okay," Brutal said. "I'm just jumpy, that's all."

"Me too," Harry said stiffly. "Now if this cussed old thing will just start—"

He walked around the hood of the truck, still muttering, and Brutal tipped me a wink. As far as Coffey was concerned, we had ceased to exist. His head was tilted back and he was drinking in the sight of the stars sprawling across the sky.

"I'll ride in back with him, if you want," Brutal offered. Behind us, the Farmall's starter whined briefly, sounding like an old dog trying to find its feet on a cold winter morning; then the engine exploded into life. Harry raced it once and let it settle into a ragged idle. "No need for both of us to do it."

"Get up front," I said. "You can ride with him on the return trip. If we don't end up making that one locked into the back of our own stagecoach, that is."

"Don't talk that way," he said, looking genuinely upset. It was as if he had realized for the first time how serious this would be for us if we were caught. "Christ, Paul!"

"Go on," I said. "In the cab."

He did as he was told. I yanked on John Coffey's arm until I could get his attention back to earth for a bit, then led him around to the rear of the truck, which was stake-sided. Harry had draped canvas over the posts, and that would be of some help if we passed cars or trucks going the other way. He hadn't been able to do anything about the open back, though.

"Upsy-daisy, big boy," I said.

"Goin for the ride now?"

"That's right."

"Good." He smiled. It was sweet and lovely, that smile, perhaps the more so because it wasn't complicated by much in the way of thought. He got up in back. I followed him, went to the front of the truckbed, and banged on top of the cab. Harry ground the transmission into first and the truck pulled out of the little bower he had hidden it in, shaking and juddering.

John Coffey stood spread-legged in the middle of the truckbed, head cocked up at the stars again, smiling broadly, unmindful of the boughs that whipped at him as Harry turned his truck toward the highway. "Look, boss!" he cried in a low, rapturous voice, pointing up into the black night. "It's Cassie, the lady in the rockin chair!"

He was right; I could see her in the lane of stars between the dark bulk of the passing trees. But it wasn't Cassiopeia I thought of when he spoke of the lady in the rocking chair; it was Melinda Moores.

"I see her, John," I said, and tugged on his arm. "But you have to sit down now, all right?"

He sat with his back against the cab, never taking his eyes off the night sky. On his face was a look of sublime unthinking happiness. The Green Mile fell farther behind us with each revolution of the Farmall's bald tires, and for the time being, at least, the seemingly endless flow of John Coffey's tears had stopped.

7

It was twenty-five miles to Hal Moores's house on Chimney Ridge, and in Harry Terwilliger's slow and rattly farm truck, the trip took over an hour. It was an eerie ride, and although it seems to me now that every moment of it is still etched in my memory—every turn, every bump, every dip, the scary times (two of them) when trucks passed us going the other way—I don't think I could come even close to describing how I felt, sitting back there with John Coffey, both of us bundled up like Indians in the old blankets Harry had been thoughtful enough to bring along.

It was, most of all, a sense of *lostness*—the deep and terrible ache a child feels when he realizes he has gone wrong somewhere, all the landmarks are strange, and he no longer knows how to find his way home. I was out in the night with a prisoner—not just *any* prisoner, but one who had been tried and convicted for the murder of two little girls, and sentenced to die for the crime. My belief that he was innocent wouldn't matter if we were caught; we would go to jail ourselves, and probably Dean Stanton would, too. I had thrown over a life of work and belief because of one bad execution and because I believed the overgrown lummox sitting beside me *might* be able to cure a woman's inoperable brain tumor. Yet watching John watch the stars, I realized with dismay that I no longer *did* believe that, if I ever really had; my urinary infection seemed faraway and unimportant now, as such harsh and painful things always do once they are past (if a woman could really remember how bad it hurt to have her first baby, my mother once said, she'd never have a second). As for Mr. Jingles, wasn't it possible, even likely, that we had been wrong about how badly Percy had hurt him? Or that John—who really did have some kind of hypnotic power, there was no doubt of that much, at least—had somehow fooled us into thinking we'd seen something we hadn't seen at all? Then there was the matter of Hal Moores. On the day I'd surprised him in his office, I'd encountered a palsied, weepy old man. But I didn't think that was the truest side of the warden. I thought the real Warden Moores was the man who'd once broken the wrist of a skatehound who tried to stab him; the man who had pointed out to me with cynical accuracy that Delacroix's nuts were going to cook no matter who was out front on the execution team. Did I think that Hal Moores would stand meekly aside and let us bring a convicted child-murderer into his house to lay hands on his wife?

My doubt grew like a sickness as we rode along. I simply did not understand why I had done the things I had, or why I'd persuaded the others to go along with me on this crazy night journey, and I did not believe we had a chance of getting away with it—not a hound's chance of heaven, as the oldtimers used to say. Yet I made no effort to cry it off, either, which I might have been able to do; things wouldn't pass irrevocably out of our hands until we showed up at Moores's house. Something—I think it might have been no more than the waves of exhilaration coming off the giant sitting next to me—kept me from hammering on top of the cab and yelling at Harry to turn around and go back to the prison while there was still time.

Such was my frame of mind as we passed off the highway and onto County 5, and from County 5 onto Chimney Ridge Road. Some fifteen minutes after that, I saw the shape of a roof blotting out the stars and knew we had arrived.

Harry shifted down from second to low (I think he only made it all the way into top gear once during the whole trip). The engine lugged, sending a shudder through the whole truck, as if it, too, dreaded what now lay directly ahead of us.

Harry swung into Moores's gravelled driveway and parked the grumbling truck behind the warden's sensible black Buick. Ahead and slightly to our right was a neat-as-a-pin house in the style which I believe is called Cape Cod. That sort of house should have looked out of place in our ridge country, perhaps, but it didn't. The moon had come up, its grin a little fatter this morning, and by its light I could see that the yard, always so beautifully kept, now looked uncared for. It was just leaves, mostly, that hadn't been raked away. Under normal circumstances that would have been Melly's job, but Melly hadn't been up to any leaf-raking this fall, and she would never see the leaves fall again. That was the truth of the matter, and I had been mad to think this vacant-eyed idiot could change it.

Maybe it still wasn't too late to save ourselves, though. I made as if to get up, the blanket I'd been wearing slipping off my shoulders. I would lean over, tap on the driver's-side window, tell Harry to get the hell out before—

John Coffey grabbed my forearm in one of his hamhock fists, pulling me back down as effortlessly as I might have done to a toddler. "Look, boss," he said, pointing. "Someone's up."

I followed the direction of his finger and felt a sinking—not just of the belly, but of the heart. There was a spark of light in one of the back windows. The room where Melinda now spent her days and nights, most likely; she would be no more capable of using the stairs than she would of going out to rake the leaves which had fallen during the recent storm.

They'd heard the truck, of course—Harry Terwilliger's goddam Farmall, its engine bellowing and farting down the length of an exhaust pipe unencumbered by anything so frivolous as a muffler. Hell, the Mooreses probably weren't sleeping that well these nights, anyway.

A light closer to the front of the house went on (the kitchen), then the living-room overhead, then the one in the front hall, then the one over the stoop. I watched these forward-marching lights the way a man standing against a cement wall and smoking his last cigarette might watch the lockstep approach of the firing squad. Yet I did not entirely acknowledge to myself even then that it was too late until the uneven chop of the Farmall's engine faded into silence, and the doors creaked, and the gravel crunched as Harry and Brutal got out.

John was up, pulling me with him. In the dim light, his face looked lively and eager. Why not? I remember thinking. Why shouldn't he look eager? He's a fool.

Brutal and Harry were standing shoulder to shoulder at the foot of the truck, like kids in a thunderstorm, and I saw that both of them looked as scared, confused, and uneasy as I felt. That made me feel even worse.

John got down. For him it was more of a step than a jump. I followed, stiff-legged and miserable. I would have sprawled on the cold gravel if he hadn't caught me by the arm.

"This is a mistake," Brutal said in a hissy little voice. His eyes were very wide and very frightened. "Christ Almighty, Paul, what were we thinking?"

"Too late now," I said. I pushed one of Coffey's hips, and he went obediently enough to stand beside Harry. Then I grabbed Brutal's elbow like this was a date we were on and got the two of us walking toward the stoop where that light was now burning. "Let me do the talking. Understand?"

"Yeah," Brutal said. "Right now that's just about the only thing I *do* understand."

I looked back over my shoulder. "Harry, stay by

the truck with him until I call for you. I don't want Moores to see him until I'm ready." Except I was never going to be ready. I knew that now.

Brutal and I had just reached the foot of the steps when the front door was hauled open hard enough to flap the brass knocker against its plate. There stood Hal Moores in blue pajama pants and a strap-style tee-shirt, his iron-gray hair standing up in tufts and twists. He was a man who had made a thousand enemies over the course of his career, and he knew it. Clasped in his right hand, the abnormally long barrel not quite pointing at the floor, was the pistol which had always been mounted over the mantel. It was the sort of gun known as a Ned Buntline Special, it had been his grandfather's, and right then (I saw this with a further sinking in my gut) it was fully cocked.

"Who the hell goes there at two-thirty in the god-dam morning?" he asked. I heard no fear at all in his voice. And—for the time being, at least—his shakes had stopped. The hand holding the gun was as steady as a stone. "Answer me, or—" The barrel of the gun began to rise.

"Stop it, Warden!" Brutal raised his hands, palms out, toward the man with the gun. I have never heard his voice sound the way it did then; it was as if the shakes turned out of Moores's hands had some-how found their way into Brutus Howell's throat. "It's us! It's Paul and me and ... it's us!"

He took the first step up, so that the light over the stoop could fall fully on his face. I joined him. Hal Moores looked back and forth between us, his angry determination giving way to bewilderment. "What are you doing here?" he asked. "Not only is it the shank of the morning, you boys have the duty. I know you do, I've got the roster pinned up in my workshop. So what in the name of . . . oh, Jesus. It's not a lockdown, is it? Or a riot?" He looked between us, and his gaze sharpened. "Who else is down by that truck?"

Let me do the talking. So I had instructed Brutal, but now the time to talk was here and I couldn't even open my mouth. On my way into work that afternoon I had carefully planned out what I was going to say when we got here, and had thought that it didn't sound too crazy. Not normal—nothing about it was normal—but maybe *close enough* to normal to get us through the door and give us a chance. Give *John* a chance. But now all my carefully rehearsed words were lost in a roaring confusion. Thoughts and images—Del burning, the mouse dying, Toot jerking in Old Sparky's lap and screaming that he was a done tom turkey—whirled inside my head like sand caught in a dust-devil. I believe there is good in the world, all of it flowing in one way or another from a loving God. But I believe there's another force as well, one every bit as real as the God I have prayed to my whole life, and that it works consciously to bring all our decent impulses to ruin. Not Satan, I don't mean Satan (although I believe he is real, too), but a kind of demon of discord, a prankish and stupid thing that laughs with glee when an old man sets himself on fire trying to light his pipe or when a much-loved baby puts its first Christmas toy in its mouth and chokes to death on it. I've had a lot of years to think on this, all the way from Cold Mountain to Georgia Pines, and I believe that force was actively at work among us on that morning, swirling everywhere like a fog, trying to keep John Coffey away from Melinda Moores.

"Warden ... Hal ... I ..." Nothing I tried made any sense.

He raised the pistol again, pointing it between Brutal and me, not listening. His bloodshot eyes had gotten very wide. And here came Harry Terwilliger, being more or less pulled along by our big boy, who was wearing his wide and daffily charming smile.

"Coffey," Moores breathed. "John Coffey." He pulled in breath and yelled in a voice that was reedy but strong: "Halt! Halt right there, or I shoot!"

From somewhere behind him, a weak and wavery female voice called: "Hal? What are you doing out there? Who are you talking to, you fucking cocksucker?"

He turned in that direction for just a moment, his face confused and despairing. Just a moment, as I say, but it should have been long enough for me to snatch the long-barrelled gun out of his hand. Except I couldn't lift my own hands. They might have had weights tied to them. My head seemed full of static, like a radio trying to broadcast during an electrical storm. The only emotions I remember feeling were fright and a kind of dull embarrassment for Hal.

Harry and John Coffey reached the foot of the steps. Moores turned away from the sound of his wife's voice and raised the gun again. He said later that yes, he fully intended to shoot Coffey; he suspected we were all prisoners, and that the brains behind whatever was happening were back by the truck, lurking in the shadows. He didn't understand why we should have been brought to his house, but revenge seemed the most likely possibility.

Before he could shoot, Harry Terwilliger stepped up ahead of Coffey and then moved in front of him, shielding most of his body. Coffey didn't make him do it; Harry did it on his own.

"No, Warden Moores!" he said. "It's all right! No one's armed, no one's going to get hurt, we're here to help!"

"Help?" Moores's tangled, tufted eyebrows drew together. His eyes blazed. I couldn't take my eyes off the cocked hammer of the Buntline. "Help *what*? Help *who*?"

As if in answer, the old woman's voice rose again, querulous and certain and utterly lost: "Come in here and poke my mudhole, you son of a bitch! Bring your asshole friends, too! Let them all have a turn!"

I looked at Brutal, shaken to my soul. I'd understood that she swore—that the tumor was somehow *making* her swear—but this was more than swearing. A lot more.

"What are you doing here?" Moores asked us again. A lot of the determination had gone out of his voice—his wife's wavering cries had done that. "I don't understand. Is it a prison break, or . . ."

John set Harry aside—just picked him up and moved him over—and then climbed to the stoop. He stood between Brutal and me, so big he almost pushed us off either side and into Melly's holly bushes. Moores's eyes turned up to follow him, the way a person's eyes do when he's trying to see the top of a tall tree. And suddenly the world fell back into place for me. That spirit of discord, which had jumbled my thoughts like powerful fingers sifting through sand or grains of rice, was gone. I thought I also understood why Harry had been able to act when Brutal and I could only stand, hopeless and indecisive, in front of our boss. Harry had been with John ... and whatever spirit it is that opposes that other, demonic one, it was in John Coffey that night. And, when John stepped forward to face Warden Moores, it was that other spirit—something white, that's how I think of it, as something white—which took control of the situation. The other thing didn't leave, but I could see it drawing back like a shadow in a sudden strong light.

"I want to help," John Coffey said. Moores looked up at him, eyes fascinated, mouth hanging open. When Coffey plucked the Buntline Special from his hand and passed it to me, I don't think Hal even knew it was gone. I carefully lowered the hammer. Later, when I checked the cylinder, I would find it had been empty all along. Sometimes I wonder if Hal knew that. Meanwhile, John was still murmuring. "I came to help her. Just to help. That's all I want."

"Hal!" she cried from the back bedroom. Her voice sounded a little stronger now, but it also sounded afraid, as if the thing which had so confused and unmanned us had now retreated to her. "Make them go away, whoever they are! We don't need no salesmen in the middle of the night! No Electrolux! No Hoover! No French knickers with come in the crotch! Get them out! Tell them to take a flying fuck at a rolling d . . . d . . ." Something broke—it could have been a waterglass—and then she began to sob.

"Just to help," John Coffey said in a voice so low it was hardly more than a whisper. He ignored the woman's sobbing and profanity equally. "Just to help, boss, that's all."

"You can't," Moores said. "No one can." It was a tone I'd heard before, and after a moment I realized it was how I'd sounded myself when I'd gone into Coffey's cell the night he cured my urinary infection. Hypnotized. *You mind your business and I'll mind mine* was what I'd told Delacroix . . . except it had been *Coffey* who'd been minding my business, just as he was minding Hal Moores's now.

"We think he can," Brutal said. "And we didn't risk our jobs—plus a stretch in the can ourselves, maybe—just to get here and turn around and go back without giving it the old college try."

Only I had been ready to do just that three minutes before. Brutal, too.

John Coffey took the play out of our hands. He pushed into the entry and past Moores, who raised a single strengthless hand to stop him (it trailed across Coffey's hip and fell off; I'm sure the big man never even felt it), and then shuffled down the hall toward the living room, the kitchen beyond it, and the back bedroom beyond that, where that shrill unrecognizable voice raised itself again: "You stay out of here!

Whoever you are, just stay out! I'm not dressed, my tits are out and my bitchbox is taking the breeze!"

John paid no attention, just went stolidly along, head bent so he wouldn't smash any of the light fixtures, his round brown skull gleaming, his hands swinging at his sides. After a moment we followed him, me first, Brutal and Hal side by side, and Harry bringing up the rear. I understood one thing perfectly well: it was all out of our hands now, and in John's.

8

The woman in the back bedroom, propped up against the headboard and staring wall-eyed at the giant who had come into her muddled sight, didn't look at all like the Melly Moores I had known for twenty years; she didn't even look like the Melly Moores Janice and I had visited shortly before Delacroix's execution. The woman propped up in that bed looked like a sick child got up as a Halloween witch. Her livid skin was a hanging dough of wrinkles. It was puckered up around the eye on the right side, as if she were trying to wink. That same side of her mouth turned down; one old yellow eyetooth hung out over her liverish lower lip. Her hair was a wild thin fog around her skull. The room stank of the stuff our bodies dispose of with such decorum when things are running right. The chamberpot by her bed was half full of some vile yellowish goo. We had come too late anyway, I thought, horrified. It had only been a matter of days since she had been recognizable—sick but still herself. Since then, the thing in her head must have moved with horrifying speed to consolidate its position. I didn't think even John Coffey could help her now.

Her expression when Coffey entered was one of fear and horror—as if something inside her had recognized a doctor that might be able to get at it and pry it loose, after all . . . to sprinkle salt on it the way you do on a leech to make it let go its grip. Hear me carefully: I'm not saying that Melly Moores was possessed, and I'm aware that, wrought up as I was, all my perceptions of that night must be suspect. But I have never completely discounted the possibility of demonic possession, either. There was something in her eyes, I tell you, something that looked like fear. On that I think you *can* trust me; it's an emotion I've seen too much of to mistake.

Whatever it was, it was gone in a hurry, replaced by a look of lively, irrational interest. That unspeakable mouth trembled in what might have been a smile.

"Oh, so big!" she cried. She sounded like a little girl just coming down with a bad throat infection. She took her hands—as spongy-white as her face—out from under the counterpane and patted them together. "Pull down your pants! I've heard about nigger-cocks my whole life but never seen one!"

Behind me, Moores made a soft groaning sound, full of despair.

John Coffey paid no attention to any of it. After standing still for a moment, as if to observe her from a little distance, he crossed to the bed, which was illuminated by a single bedside lamp. It threw a bright circle of light on the white counterpane drawn up to the lace at the throat of her nightgown. Beyond the bed, in shadow, I saw the chaise longue which belonged in the parlor. An afghan Melly had knitted with her own hands in happier days lay half on the chaise and half on the floor. It was here Hal had been sleeping—dozing, at least—when we pulled in.

As John approached, her expression underwent a third change. Suddenly I saw Melly, whose kindness had meant so much to me over the years, and even more to Janice when the kids had flown from the nest and she had been left feeling so alone and useless and blue. Melly was still interested, but now her interest seemed sane and aware.

"Who are you?" she asked in a clear, reasonable voice. "And why have you so many scars on your hands and arms? Who hurt you so badly?"

"I don't hardly remember where they all come from, ma'am," John Coffey said in a humble voice, and sat down beside her on her bed.

Melinda smiled as well as she could—the sneering right side of her mouth trembled, but wouldn't quite come up. She touched a white scar, curved like a scimitar, on the back of his left hand. "What a blessing that is! Do you understand why?"

"Reckon if you don't know who hurt you or dog you down, it don't keep you up nights," John Coffey said in his almost-Southern voice.

She laughed at that, the sound as pure as silver in the bad-smelling sickroom. Hal was beside me now, breathing rapidly but not trying to interfere. When Melly laughed, his rapid breathing paused for a moment, indrawn, and one of his big hands gripped my shoulder. He gripped it hard enough to leave a bruise—I saw it the next day—but right then I hardly felt it.

"What's your name?" she asked.

"John Coffey, ma'am."

"Coffey like the drink."

"Yes, ma'am, only spelled different."

She lay back against her pillows, propped up but not quite sitting up, looking at him. He sat beside her, looking back, and the light from the lamp circled them like they were actors on a stage—the hulking black man in the prison overall and the small dying white woman. She stared into John's eyes with shining fascination.

"Ma'am?"

"Yes, John Coffey?" The words barely breathed, barely slipping to us on the bad-smelling air. I felt the muscles bunching on my arms and legs and back. Somewhere, far away, I could feel the warden clutching my arm, and to the side of my vision I could see Harry and Brutal with their arms around each other, like little kids lost in the night. Something was going to happen. Something big. We each felt it in our own way.

John Coffey bent closer to her. The springs of the bed creaked, the bedclothes rustled, and the coldly smiling moon looked in through an upper pane of the bedroom window. Coffey's bloodshot eyes searched her upturned haggard face.

"I see it," he said. Speaking not to her—I don't think so, anyway—but to himself. "I see it, and I can help. Hold still . . . hold right still . . ."

Closer he bent, and closer still. For a moment his huge face stopped less than two inches from hers. He raised one hand off to the side, fingers splayed, as if telling something to wait ... just wait ... and then he lowered his face again. His broad, smooth lips pressed against hers and forced them open. For a moment I could see one of her eyes, staring up past Coffey, filling with an expression of what seemed to be surprise. Then his smooth bald head moved, and that was gone, too.

There was a soft whistling sound as he inhaled the air which lay deep within her lungs. That was all for a second or two, and then the floor moved under us and the whole house moved around us. It wasn't my imagination; they all felt it, they all remarked on it later. It was a kind of rippling thump. There was a crash as something very heavy fell over in the parlor—the grandfather clock, it turned out to be. Hal Moores tried to have it repaired, but it never kept time for more than fifteen minutes at a stretch again.

Closer by there was a crack followed by a tinkle as the pane of glass through which the moon had been peeking broke. A picture on the wall—a clipper ship cruising one of the seven seas—fell off its hook and crashed to the floor; the glass over its front shattered.

I smelled something hot and saw smoke rising from the bottom of the white counterpane which covered her. A portion was turning black, down by the jittering lump that was her right foot. Feeling like a man in a dream, I shook free of Moores's hand and stepped to the night-table. There was a glass of water there, surrounded by three or four bottles of pills which had fallen over during the shake. I picked up the water and dumped it on the place that was smoking. There was a hiss.

John Coffey went on kissing her in that deep and intimate way, inhaling and inhaling, one hand still held out, the other on the bed, propping up his immense weight. The fingers were splayed; the hand looked to me like a brown starfish.

Suddenly, her back arched. One of her own hands flailed out in the air, the fingers clenching and unclenching in a series of spasms. Her feet drummed against the bed. Then something screamed. Again, that's not just me; the other men heard it, as well. To Brutal it sounded like a wolf or coyote with its leg caught in a trap. To me it sounded like an eagle, the way you'd sometimes hear them on still mornings back then, cruising down through the misty cuts with their wings stiffly spread.

Outside, the wind gusted hard enough to give the house a second shake—and that was strange, you know, because until then there had been no wind to speak of at all.

John Coffey pulled away from her, and I saw that her face had smoothed out. The right side of her mouth no longer drooped. Her eyes had regained their normal shape, and she looked ten years younger. He regarded her raptly for a moment or two, and then he began to cough. He turned his head so as not to cough in her face, lost his balance (which wasn't hard; big as he was, he'd been sitting with his butt halfway off the side of the bed to start with), and went down onto the floor. There was enough of him to give the house a third shake. He landed on his knees and hung his head over, coughing like a man in the last stages of TB.

I thought, *Now the bugs. He's going to cough them out, and what a lot there'll be this time.*

But he didn't. He only went on coughing in deep retching barks, hardly finding time between fits to snatch in the next breath of air. His dark, chocolatey skin was graying out. Alarmed, Brutal went to him, dropped to one knee beside him, and put an arm across his broad, spasming back. As if Brutal's moving had broken a spell, Moores went to his wife's bed and sat where Coffey had sat. He hardly seemed to register the coughing, choking giant's presence at all. Although Coffey was kneeling at his very feet, Moores had eyes only for his wife, who was gazing at him with amazement. Looking at her was like looking at a dirty mirror which has been wiped clean.

"John!" Brutal shouted. "Sick it up! Sick it up like you done before!"

John went on barking those choked coughs. His eyes were wet, not with tears but with strain. Spit flew from his mouth in a fine spray, but nothing else came out.

Brutal whammed him on the back a couple of times, then looked around at me. "He's choking! Whatever he sucked out of her, he's choking on it!"

I started forward. Before I got two steps, John knee-walked away from me and into the corner of the room, still coughing harshly and dragging for each breath. He laid his forehead against the wall-paper—wild red roses overspreading a garden wall—and made a gruesome deep hacking sound, as if he were trying to vomit up the lining of his own throat. That'll bring the bugs if anything can, I remember thinking, but there was no sign of them. All the same, his coughing fit seemed to ease a little.

"I'm all right, boss," he said, still leaning with his forehead against the wild roses. His eyes remained closed. I'm not sure how he knew I was there, but he clearly did. "Honest I am. See to the lady."

I looked at him doubtfully, then turned to the bed. Hal was stroking Melly's brow, and I saw an amazing thing above it: some of her hair—not very much, but some—had gone back to black.

"What's happened?" she asked him. As I watched, color began to blush into her cheeks. It was as if she had stolen a couple of roses right out of the wallpaper. "How did I get here? We were going to the hospital up in Indianola, weren't we? A doctor was going to shoot X-rays into my head and take pictures of my brain."

"Shhh," Hal said. "Shhh, dearie, none of that matters now."

"But I don't *understand*!" she nearly wailed. "We stopped at a roadside stand . . . you bought me a dime packet of posies . . . and then . . . I'm here. It's dark! Have you had your supper, Hal? Why am I in the guest room? Did I have the X-ray?" Her eyes moved across Harry almost without seeing him—that was shock, I imagine—and fixed on me. "Paul? Did I have the X-ray?"

"Yes," I said. "It was clear."

"They didn't find a tumor?"

"No," I said. "They say the headaches will likely stop now."

Beside her, Hal burst into tears.

She sat forward and kissed his temple. Then her eyes moved to the corner. "Who is that Negro man? Why is he in the corner?"

I turned and saw John trying to get up on his feet. Brutal helped him and John made it with a final lunge. He stood facing the wall, though, like a child who has been bad. He was still coughing in spasms, but these seemed to be weakening now.

"John," I said. "Turn around, big boy, and see this lady."

He slowly turned. His face was still the color of ashes, and he looked ten years older, like a once powerful man at last losing a long battle with consumption. His eyes were cast down on his prison slippers, and he looked as if he wished for a hat to wring.

"Who are you?" she asked again. "What's your name?"

"John Coffey, ma'am," he said, to which she immediately replied, "But not spelled like the drink."

Hal started beside her. She felt it, and patted his hand reassuringly without taking her eyes from the black man.

"I dreamed of you," she said in a soft, wondering voice. "I dreamed you were wandering in the dark, and so was I. We found each other."

John Coffey said nothing.

"We found each other in the dark," she said. "Stand up, Hal, you're pinning me in here."

He got up and watched with disbelief as she turned back the counterpane. "Melly, you can't—"

"Don't be silly," she said, and swung her legs out. "Of course I can." She smoothed her nightgown, stretched, then got to her feet.

"My God," Hal whispered. "My dear God in heaven, *look* at her."

She went to John Coffey. Brutal stood away from her, an awed expression on his face. She limped with the first step, did no more than favor her right leg a bit with the second, and then even that was gone. I remembered Brutal handing the colored spool to Delacroix and saying, "Toss it—I want to see how he runs." Mr. Jingles had limped then, but on the next night, the night Del walked the Mile, he had been fine.

Melly put her arms around John and hugged him. Coffey stood there for a moment, letting himself be hugged, and then he raised one hand and stroked the top of her head. This he did with infinite gentleness. His face was still gray. I thought he looked dreadfully sick.

She stood away from him, her face turned up to his. "Thank you."

"Right welcome, ma'am."

She turned to Hal and walked back to him. He put his arms around her.

"Paul—" It was Harry. He held his right wrist out to me and tapped the face of his watch. It was pressing on to three o'clock. Light would start showing by four-thirty. If we wanted to get Coffey back to Cold Mountain before that happened, we would have to go soon. And I wanted to get him back. Partly because the longer this went on the worse our chances of getting away with it became, yes, of course. But I also wanted John in a place where I could legitimately call a doctor for him, if the need arose. Looking at him, I thought it might.

The Mooreses were sitting on the edge of the bed, arms around each other. I thought of asking Hal out into the living room for a private word, then realized I could ask until the cows came home and he wouldn't budge from where he was right then. He might be able to take his eyes off her—for a few seconds, at least—by the time the sun came up, but not now.

"Hal," I said. "We have to go now."

He nodded, not looking at me. He was studying the color in his wife's cheeks, the natural unstrained curve of his wife's lips, the new black in his wife's hair.

I tapped him on the shoulder, hard enough to get his attention for a moment, at least.

"Hal, we never came here."

"What—?"

"We never came here," I said. "Later on we'll talk, but for now that's all you need to know. We were never here."

"Yes, all right . . ." He forced himself to focus on me for a moment, with what was clearly an effort. "You got him out. Can you get him back in?"

"I think so. Maybe. But we need to go."

"How did you know he could do this?" Then he

shook his head, as if realizing for himself that this wasn't the time. "Paul ... thank you."

"Don't thank me," I said. "Thank John."

He looked at John Coffey, then put out one hand— just as I had done on the day Harry and Percy escorted John onto the block. "Thank you. Thank you so much."

John looked at the hand. Brutal threw a none-too-subtle elbow into his side. John started, then took the hand and gave it a shake. Up, down, back to center, release. "Welcome," he said in a hoarse voice. It sounded to me like Melly's when she had clapped her hands and told John to pull down his pants. "Welcome," he said to the man who would, in the ordinary course of things, grasp a pen with that hand and then sign John Coffey's execution order with it.

Harry tapped the face of his watch, more urgently this time.

"Brute?" I said. "Ready?"

"Hello, Brutus," Melinda said in a cheerful voice, as if noticing him for the first time. "It's good to see you. Would you gentlemen like tea? Would you, Hal? I could make it." She got up again. "I've been ill, but I feel fine now. Better than I have in years."

"Thank you, Missus Moores, but we have to go," Brutal said. "It's past John's bedtime." He smiled to show it was a joke, but the look he gave John was as anxious as I felt.

"Well ... if you're sure ..."

"Yes, ma'am. Come on, John Coffey." He tugged John's arm to get him going, and John went.

"Just a minute!" Melinda shook free of Hal's hand

and ran as lightly as a girl to where John stood. She put her arms around him and gave him another hug. Then she reached around to the nape of her neck and pulled a fine-link chain out of her bodice. At the end of it was a silver medallion. She held it out to John, who looked at it uncomprehendingly.

"It's St. Christopher," she said. "I want you to have it, Mr. Coffey, and wear it. He'll keep you safe. Please wear it. For me."

John looked at me, troubled, and I looked at Hal, who first spread his hands and then nodded.

"Take it, John," I said. "It's a present."

John took it, slipped the chain around his bull-neck, and dropped the St. Christopher medallion into the front of his shirt. He had completely stopped coughing now, but I thought he looked grayer and sicker than ever.

"Thank you, ma'am," he said.

"No," she replied. "Thank *you*. Thank *you*, John Coffey."

9

I rode up in the cab with Harry going back, and was damned glad to be there. The heater was broken, but we were out of the open air, at least. We had gone about ten miles when Harry spotted a little turnout and veered the truck into it.

"What is it?" I asked. "Is it a bearing?" To my mind, the problem could have been that or anything; every component of the Farmall's engine and transmission sounded on the verge of going cataclysmically wrong or giving up the ghost entirely.

"Nope," Harry said, sounding apologetic. "I got to take a leak, is all. My back teeth are floatin."

It turned out that we all did, except for John. When Brutal asked if he wouldn't like to step down and help us water the bushes, he just shook his head without looking up. He was leaning against the back of the cab and wearing one of the Army blankets over his shoulders like a serape. I couldn't get any kind of read on his complexion, but I could hear his breathing—dry and raspy, like wind blowing through straw. I didn't like it.

I walked into a clump of willows, unbuttoned, and

let go. I was still close enough to my urinary infection so that the body's amnesia had not taken full hold, and I could be grateful simply to be able to pee without needing to scream. I stood there, emptying out and looking up at the moon; I was hardly aware of Brutal standing next to me and doing the same thing until he said in a low voice, "He'll never sit in Old Sparky."

I looked around at him, surprised and a little frightened by the low certainty in his tone. "What do you mean?"

"I mean he swallered that stuff instead of spitting out like he done before for a reason. It might take a week—he's awful big and strong—but I bet it's quicker. One of us'll do a check-tour and there he'll be, lying dead as stone on his bunk."

I'd thought I was done peeing, but at that a little shiver twisted up my back and a little more squirted out. As I rebuttoned my fly, I thought that what Brutal was saying made perfect sense. And I hoped, all in all, that he was right. John Coffey didn't deserve to die at all, if I was right in my reasoning about the Detterick girls, but if he *did* die, I didn't want it to be by my hand. I wasn't sure I could lift my hand to do it, if it came to that.

"Come on," Harry murmured out of the dark. "It's gettin late. Let's get this done."

As we walked back to the truck, I realized we had left John entirely alone—stupidity on the Percy Wetmore level. I thought that he would be gone; that he'd spat out the bugs as soon as he saw he was unguarded, and had then just lit out for the territories, like Huck and Jim on the Big Muddy. All we would find was the blanket he had been wearing around his shoulders.

But he was there, still sitting with his back against the cab and his forearms propped on his knees. He looked up at the sound of our approach and tried to give us a smile. It hung there for a moment on his haggard face and then slipped off.

"How you doing, Big John?" Brutal asked, climbing into the back of the truck again and retrieving his own blanket.

"Fine, boss," John said listlessly. "I's fine."

Brutal patted his knee. "We'll be back soon. And when we get squared away, you know what? I'm going to see you get a great big cup of hot coffee. Sugar and cream, too."

You bet, I thought, going around to the passenger side of the cab and climbing in. If we don't get arrested and thrown in jail ourselves first.

But I'd been living with that idea ever since we'd thrown Percy into the restraint room, and it didn't worry me enough to keep me awake. I dozed off and dreamed of Calvary Hill. Thunder in the west and a smell that might have been juniper berries. Brutal and Harry and Dean and I were standing around in robes and tin hats like in a Cecil B. DeMille movie. We were Centurions, I guess. There were three crosses, Percy Wetmore and Eduard Delacroix flanking John Coffey. I looked down at my hand and saw I was holding a bloody hammer.

We got to get him down from there, Paul! Brutal screamed. *We got to get him down!*

Except we couldn't, they'd taken away the stepladder. I started to tell Brutal this, and then an extra-hard jounce of the truck woke me up. We were backing into the place where Harry had hidden the truck earlier on a day that already seemed to stretch back to the beginning of time.

The two of us got out and went around to the back. Brutal hopped down all right, but John Coffey's knees buckled and he almost fell. It took all three of us to catch him, and he was no more than set solid on his feet again before he went off into another of those coughing fits, this one the worst yet. He bent over, the coughing sounds muffled by the heels of his palms, which he held pressed against his mouth.

When his coughing eased, we covered the front of the Farmall with the pine boughs again and walked back the way we had come. The worst part of that whole surreal furlough was—for me, at least—the last two hundred yards, with us scurrying back south along the shoulder of the highway. I could see (or thought I could) the first faint lightening of the sky in the east, and felt sure some early farmer, out to harvest his pumpkins or dig his last few rows of yams, would come along and see us. And even if that didn't happen, we would hear someone (in my imagination it sounded like Curtis Anderson) shout *"Hold it right there!"* as I used the Aladdin key to unlock the enclosure around the bulkhead leading to the tunnel. Then two dozen carbine-toting guards would step out of the woods and our little adventure would be over.

By the time we actually got to the enclosure, my heart was whamming so hard that I could see little white dots exploding in front of my eyes with each pulse it made. My hands felt cold and numb and faraway, and for the longest time I couldn't get the key to go into the lock.

"Oh Christ, headlights!" Harry moaned.

I looked up and saw brightening fans of light on the road. My keyring almost fell out of my hand; I managed to clutch it at the last second.

"Give them to me," Brutal said. "I'll do it."

"No, I've got it," I said. The key at last slipped into its slot and turned. A moment later we were in. We crouched behind the bulkhead and watched as a Sunshine Bread truck went pottering past the prison. Beside me I could hear John Coffey's tortured breathing. He sounded like an engine which has almost run out of oil. He had held the bulkhead door up effortlessly for us on our way out, but we didn't even ask him to help this time; it would have been out of the question. Brutal and I got the door up, and Harry led John down the steps. The big man tottered as he went, but he got down. Brutal and I followed him as fast as we could, then lowered the bulkhead behind us and locked it again.

"Christ, I think we're gonna—" Brutal began, but I cut him off with a sharp elbow to the ribs.

"Don't say it," I said. "Don't even think it, until he's safe back in his cell."

"And there's Percy to think about," Harry said. Our voices had a flat, echoey quality in the brick tunnel. "The evening ain't over as long as we got him to contend with."

As it turned out, our evening was *far* from over.

To Be Concluded

The serial thriller
concludes next month . . .

STEPHEN KING'S
THE GREEN MILE:
Part Six
Coffey On the Mile

Cold Mountain Penitentiary has seen its share of death through the years. Now it's John Coffey's turn to take that final walk down the Green Mile. Yet prison guard Paul Edgecombe has uncovered a devastating truth, which means he could be too late to save both himself and Coffey.

Don't miss the dramatic conclusion!

Also available:

Visit *The Green Mile* on the Internet!
http://www.greenmile.com

Escaping a madman was the easy part . . .

ROSE MADDER
by Stephen king

Rose Daniels saw the single drop of blood on the bed sheet—and knew she must escape from her macabre marriage before it was too late. But tracking Rose is her sadistic cop of a husband, Norman, a terrifying monster and a savage brute. The only place Rose has found to hide could be the most dangerous of all . . .

Available Now
A Signet Paperback

Return to a world of extraordinary vision . . .

THE DARK TOWER IV
Wizard and Glass
by Stephen King

The epic journey of Roland the Gunslinger continues in this long-awaited fourth volume. Find out what happens after Roland and his friends Susannah and Eddie begin their amazing ride out of the city and into the realms of a world still unexplored . . .

Available Summer 1997
A Plume Trade Paperback

Welcome to the loneliest highway,
and the deadliest ...

DESPERATION

by Stephen King

Just off Route 50 in Nevada lies the small
mining town of Desperation, where a local
cop has suddenly turned anything but law-
man. His victims were the lucky ones. But for
a small group of survivors, desperation is no
longer just the name of a town—it's a state of
mind. And it will take an extraordinary
young boy to lead them through a living
nightmare.

Coming in September 1996
A Viking Hardcover Book

*The suburbs have never been
more terrifying . . .*

THE REGULATORS

by Richard Bachman

It's a summer afternoon in Wentworth, Ohio,
and on Poplar Street, everything's normal . . .
except for the red van idling just up the hill.
Soon it will begin to roll, and the madness
will begin. And by the time night falls, the
surviving residents will find themselves in another world, one where anything is possible
. . . and where The Regulators are on their
way.

Coming in September 1996
A Dutton Hardcover Book

Win an Autographed Stephen King Library!

Enter
THE GREEN MILE Contest!

6 winners per month will receive an autographed GREEN MILE manuscript (36 winners total). All winners are then eligible for the Grand Prize— an autographed Stephen King library!

See reverse side for details.

Name _____

Address _____

City _____

State_____ Zip Code _____

To enter:

1. Answer the following question:

   The narrator, Paul Edgecombe, has a strange dream on the way back from Warden Moores' house. What do you think the dream means?

2. Write your answer on a separate piece of paper (in 50 words or less)

3. Mail to: **THE GREEN MILE PART 5 CONTEST, P.O. Box 9035, Medford, NY, 11763**

OFFICIAL RULES

1. To enter, hand print your name and complete address on the official entry form (original, photocopy, or a plain piece of paper). Then, on a separate piece of paper (no larger than 8-1/2" x 11") in 50 words or less, hand-printed or typed, complete the following statement:

The narrator, Paul Edgecombe, has a strange dream on the way back from Warden Moores' house. What do you think the dream means?

Staple your statement to your entry form and mail to: THE GREEN MILE PART 5 CONTEST, P.O. Box 9035, Medford, NY 11763. Entries must be received by September 30, 1996, to be eligible. Not responsible for late, lost, misdirected mail or printing errors.

2. All entries will be judged by Marden-Kane, Inc., an independent judging organization in conjunction with Penguin USA based upon the following criteria: Originality 35%, Content 35%, Sincerity 20%, and Clarity 10%. By entering this contest, entrants accept and agree to be bound to these rules and the decisions of the judges which shall be final and binding. All entries become the property of the sponsor and will not be acknowledged or returned. Each entry must be the original work of the entrant. Winners will be notified by mail and may be required to execute an affidavit of eligibility and release which must be returned within 14 days of notification or an alternate winner will be selected.

3. PRIZES: Six (6) winners for each part of THE GREEN MILE will receive a manuscript of THE GREEN MILE autographed by Stephen King (36 winners total). Approximate retail value: $100.00. All winners in subsequent GREEN MILE contests are eligible to win a Grand Prize of an autographed Stephen King library. Approximate retail value: $1000.00. Grand Prize will be awarded after November 29, 1996, based upon criteria outlined above.

4. Contest open to residents of the United States and Canada 18 years of age and older, except employees and the immediate families of Penguin USA, its affiliates, subsidiaries, advertising agencies, and Marden-Kane, Inc. Void in FL, VT, MD, AZ, the Province of Quebec, and wherever else prohibited by law. All Federal, State, Local, and Provincial laws apply. Taxes, if any, are the sole responsibility of the prize winners. If winners are Canadian, he/she will be required to answer an arithmetical skill testing question administered by mail. Winners consent to the use of their name and/or photos or likeness for advertising purposes without additional compensation (except where prohibited).

5. For the names of the major prize winners, send a self-addressed, stamped envelope after September 30, 1996, to: THE GREEN MILE CONTEST WINNER, P.O. Box 5000, Manhasset, NY, 11030.

Ⓟ Signet
Penguin USA • Mass Market